# DAMIAN

A DARK MAFIA ROMANCE (SANTIAGO MAFIA)

NAOMI WEST

Copyright © 2020 by Naomi West

All rights reserved.

No part of this book may be reproduced in any form or by any electronic or mechanical means, including information storage and retrieval systems, without written permission from the author, except for the use of brief quotations in a book review.

❀ Created with Vellum

# MAILING LIST

Join the Naomi West Mailing List to receive new release alerts, free giveaways, and more!

Click the link below and you'll get sent a free motorcycle club romance as a welcome present.

**JOIN NOW!** http://bit.ly/NaomiWestNewsletter

# BOOKS BY NAOMI WEST

### Dark Mafia Kingpins

*Read in any order!*

Andrei

Leon

### Dirty Dons Club

*Read in any order!*

Sergei

Luca

Vito

Nikolai

Adrik

### Bad Boy Biker's Club

*Read in any order!*

Dakota

Stryker

Kaeden

Ranger

Blade

Colt

Tank

### Outlaw Biker Brotherhood

*Read in any order!*

Devil's Revenge

Devil's Ink

Devil's Heart

Devil's Vow

Devil's Sins

Devil's Scar

**Box Sets**

Devil's Outlaws: An MC Romance Box Set

Bad Boy Bikers Club: An MC Romance Box Set

The Dirty Dons Club: A Dark Mafia Romance Box Set

**Other MC Standalones**

*Read in any order!*

Maddox

Stripped

Jace

Grinder

# DAMIAN: A DARK MAFIA ROMANCE

**Our marriage is fake. But our baby is real.**

My ex-fiancé handed me over to one of his buddies.

I'm a prop. A plaything. A fake wife.

I can tell when Damian Oakman looks at me what he wants:

Me, on my knees, begging him for faster, harder, more.

With washboard abs and an icy, piercing stare, part of me wants to give it to him.

And if I want to survive this cruise, I have to do exactly that.

I have to play the part:

Perfect wife. Perfect life.

I wanted to hate it. I wanted to hate him.

But as Damian's hardened defenses peel away one by one, so do my clothes...

And so does my resistance.

Before long, I'm the one moaning for just one more touch.

It's all a web of lies.

I don't know what's real or what's fake.

All I know is this:

I belong to the hitman now.

And nothing will ever be the same.

# 1

Piper sighed, resting her forehead on her hand and trying to think of the right words to say. She could try and go soft, but then, she had been trying to use a soft approach on Todd for weeks now, and he hadn't gotten it yet. There was no sign he was going to figure it out in the future either.

"I'm sorry," she said, finally. "I just don't think this is going to work out for us."

She expected Todd to be upset, but the chill that descended over the room surprised her. She looked up and saw that Todd's face had gone absolutely still. That sense of cold started to roll through her as well.

*Oh shit*. She had thought this break up wouldn't be that big of a deal, and that she was totally fine to do it at his place. Now, she found herself wishing they were in public, with her trying to figure out how to get a clear shot at an exit if she had to.

"What?" Todd said, his voice cold.

"I'm sorry," she said again, trying to make her voice as soft and girlish and conciliatory as she could.

*God.* She hated doing this—going all weak, limp, and harmless to try and get out of a situation, but at the same time, if it got her out, what was she really going to say?

Todd was quiet for another long moment, and then he shook his head slowly. "Tell me why."

It wasn't a question, and Piper found herself even more nervous about where this might be going.

"Todd, there isn't a single thing—"

"Bullshit," he snapped, and she couldn't contain the flinch.

Her father had yelled like that when she was small, and she'd never stopped hating the sound. The fear ran through her whipcord fast and just as strong. She'd spent years in therapy trying to shake the power that sound had over her, and she had done it so well. Almost.

"Don't yell at me," she said, but her voice sounded painfully weak.

She hated it. Hated when everything fell apart inside her head. She wanted to be brave and strong—like the Piper she had worked to be all these years—not a weak, sad, lonely little girl who didn't know what to do when her father yelled.

"Don't tell me what to do," Todd replied, but his voice was less vicious. "I'm sorry. This is just coming out of nowhere for me." He was clearly trying to make amends for the way he'd spoken.

"Todd..." She sighed, then took a deep breath. "I'm not sure how it can really come out of nowhere. I've been saying and saying that I needed more. That the way things are weren't enough. That I was lonely. You work so many hours, and it seems like we hardly see each other."

"Don't you think I would change that if I could?"

"Would you?" This time it was Piper who had snapped. "Because it seems like there are lots of opportunities for you to work a little less, but you just... never make that choice. You've broken our last four dates. I don't even remember the last time we had sex..."

His pale face was getting darker, and Piper felt the curl of fear in her stomach starting to spiral into something bigger. At least she'd stopped at home and changed into her jeans before she'd come over here; her phone was in her back pocket. If things got dicey, she could lock herself in the bathroom and call the police to come and rescue her. She should have done this in public. Or at her place, with Marissa waiting in the bedroom to back her up. One of the two. Coming to his place like this had been stupid, but it had never once occurred to her that Todd might look at her like this. Like he wanted to tear her to pieces.

*Marissa knows where I am*, Piper reminded herself. *I'm going to be okay. He might yell, but he's not going to try and kill me or anything.*

Just thinking it made her feel a little sick. A thick, smoky smell hit her nose all of a sudden, and she glanced at the stovetop.

"The garlic is burning," she said.

It was a dumb thing to say, but part of her thought that it might possibly distract him.

"I don't give a fuck about the garlic," he said, his tone higher again. "I don't care if the whole damn building burns down. I want to know what the hell is happening here. It's not about my work, and it's not about sex, and I know that, so I want you to tell me what the fuck is happening."

Another long, deep sigh, and then Piper made herself tell the truth. It sounded like the most stereotypical, stupid thing she'd ever had to say in her life, but it was the truth.

"It's about your mother," she said.

"My—" Todd burst out into laughter that had a cruel edge to it. "What the hell are you talking about?"

"The only time we see each other now is when we have dinner with your mother on Sunday night," Piper made herself say. "And then she does absolutely nothing but insinuates that she wants to see us get married before she dies and that she can't wait to meet her grandchildren."

"She's an older woman."

Piper sighed. Again. This was not the first time they had talked about his mother, but she was determined that it would be the last.

"I don't care if she's old or young. Look, I get it. You're older than me, and your mother is older too. But I'm not older. I'm 25. I don't know what I want in my life yet, not long term. I don't know if I even want to get married, if I even want kids."

"I want both," Todd said as if stating that fact was somehow relevant to her decisions.

She tried not to roll her eyes. "And I'm glad that you're sure of things for yourself. But I'm not. And I deserve the time to figure out what I want on my own, without you *or* your mother telling me what I want or trying to make my decisions for me."

Todd shook his head. "Look, I know it's confusing. I know the gig economy is messing with a lot of millennials—"

"Oh, you did not just do that."

"But if you just took a regular job, you'd settle down soon enough."

"Settle down? Really?"

"I can find you something at the firm, no problem. I think Ryan's looking for a new assistant, and if not, there's a spot for a transcriptionist down in medical billing—"

"Stop, Todd."

Todd did not stop; he listed off three more jobs, stopping just short of mentioning a secretary pool, and Piper was fairly sure that was only because there wasn't a secretary pool. If one had existed, it would have come up.

But she knew this mood. This was the Todd who didn't stop until he'd had his say. The Todd that she had thought was passionate and involved until she realized that he would use this passion to steamroll anything she said she wanted. Until she noticed how many of his rants seemed to be based on how the things she was passionate about were actually a waste of time. Just like her "little business."

"My business isn't little," she said.

Todd looked surprised. Honestly, she could give him that one; he hadn't said it this fight, just all the other ones.

"You are constantly acting like I have this stupid little hobby," she went on, "but I have a thriving business that is making a significant amount of money. I don't even have to look for clients now—people come to me to make sure their crowdfunding projects succeed. Maybe it's a little pond, but in it, I'm a pretty decent fish, and I'm happy. That's the part you don't understand, Todd, I'm happy. I like my life."

"But you don't like me."

"I like you fine. It's stupid and stereotypical to say that I hope we'll be friends. I know we won't. But it's not about me not liking you."

Todd laughed. "It's about my fucking mother."

Piper shook her head. "No, it's about us not fitting together, Todd. Not for the long term. And I don't want to lead you on. You deserve the chance to find that girl—that girl who wants to marry you and have kids, and who knows that from day one."

"But I want you." He sounded so sad and lost that she felt sorry for him for a long moment.

She stepped towards him, and then he snarled, raising his hand back, his palm open, the back of his hand facing her. She hadn't been struck since she was about three years old, but she still cowered. Girls in movies stood strong, daring someone to hit them; that wasn't Piper. She was terrified, and she didn't care if he saw it.

Seeing it might even have been what stopped him. She didn't know. She saw the look in his eyes shift, and he clenched that open hand into a fist, and then brought it down to his side. His chest was puffed out, and he looked like he was having trouble standing.

*Time to go, Piper. Get out while the getting's still, well, semi-good.*

"I'm sorry," she said again.

Her purse was on the other side of him. She thought hard about just leaving it behind and then asking him to bring it to some neutral location later. Marissa had a spare set of keys, she had cash at home, and he wasn't the type to try and do damage with her debit card to screw her over.

But then he hadn't been the type to make like he would hit her either, not until about sixty seconds ago.

She kept her head all the way down, carefully making sure that she made no eye contact, and snagged the strap of her purse. She tugged it towards her, grabbed it so that it didn't swing out and hit his leg, and took a step back as she pulled it up over her shoulder.

"I'm sorry," she said one more time as she headed for the door.

All the way across the living room, she waited to feel his hand on her shoulder, the pressure of spinning her around and turning her face directly into his fist. It would start like that, and it would end like every horror movie she'd ever seen in her life: she would be a bloody smear across his well-waxed hardwood floor.

But it didn't happen. She got to the door, threw back the deadbolt, stepped outside, and closed the door behind her. She realized that she still had his key on her keyring. She could have stood there for a minute, taking it off, and then put it back inside or even in the mailbox, but for all she knew, he was realizing at this exact minute that he'd made a mistake by letting her go. He could be running for her, ready to grab her and pull her back inside, no matter what she wanted.

*Screw it. I'll mail him the goddamn key.*

She walked away from the house and decided to call an Uber once she was at the corner. She pulled out her phone and went into her messages. She had to update Marissa. The two of them had been friends for years, and when Piper had told Marissa her plans, Marissa had been very clear that she was the emergency exit of choice. Piper had been so sure that everything was going to be fine, but Marissa had never been "Team Todd".

"This could go really bad, Piper," she'd said. "You have to be careful."

"It'll be fine, I said," Piper muttered to herself. "What could possibly go wrong, I said."

Every step she took away from Todd's townhouse was another step towards freedom. The adrenaline in her head cycled down, and she started to breathe properly again. It was something. No, it was a lot.

When she got to the coffee shop on the corner, she tapped out: *Everything's fine. Call you?*

Piper didn't actually wait for Marissa to say yes. As soon as the message said *read*, she hit dial. The phone didn't even get through the first ring before Marissa was there.

"Piper."

"Yeah. It's done."

"How did it go? Is everything okay? Are you okay?"

Piper rubbed her forehead. She didn't want to go inside the cafe and have this conversation; she would feel obliged to get a latte or something and then she'd be up all night. She felt exhausted, out of nowhere, and the only thing she wanted in the world was to get some sleep.

"Yeah, I'm fine."

If she explained that one terrifying moment, Marissa would completely lose it.

But somehow, her friend knew anyway. "Piper, what did he do? Tell me, it's okay, I'm not going to yell at him or something. I just want you safe."

All of a sudden, there were tears in Pipers' eyes. "Marissa? Can I come stay at your place for a couple of days? Maybe it sounds stupid, but I just—I don't want to go home."

There wasn't even a pause. "Of course, babe. Can you Uber over, or do you want me to come get you?"

Piper wiped her eyes. "I'll Uber; it's no big deal. Do you want me to grab anything on my way over?"

"I got wine and chocolate this afternoon. Also, an ice cream cake, just in case. I think we're good."

"Actual food? I didn't get to eat after work, and I didn't want to break up with him after a meal, you know?"

"Got it," Marissa said. "Indian or Ethiopian?"

"Indian, please. Hot."

"Make it seem like you're not crying because you're sad. Got it."

"Thank you."

"Shut up," Marissa said, her tone loving. "Get an Uber and get over here."

## 2

Damian couldn't remember the last time he had woken up normally. His heart rate was steady, he had the luxury of knowing where he was, that he was safe and calm and that he didn't need to immediately access the world around him for any potential threats. Most people would say that they'd slept like that as children. But Damian couldn't say that.

He gave a sharp inhale and held perfectly still for one long moment, assessing whether there was a particular stimulus—a noise out of place, a single footfall—that might have woken him.

He couldn't immediately identify anything and rolled onto his back, spreading his arms out over his king-size bed. In an otherwise spartan apartment, it was the luxury he allowed himself. All he did here was sleep, so he'd made sure to have an opulent bed. He could, and did, crack jokes about needing his beauty sleep, but the truth was that a tired hitman was a dead hitman, and Damian took serious pride in the work he did. It wasn't pretty, and not every man would be able to sleep with hands as bloody as his, but he'd taken dangerous men out of the world.

And innocent men too. No point in lying about that, not even to himself. Though he would sometimes allow himself to wonder—who was really innocent? How innocent were they, really? He'd never truly met an innocent man. Not deep down.

Stretching wasn't the same as lying around. Damian stood up, then went through a quick series of movements and stretches designed to loosen up his hamstrings and keep his back limber and relaxed. Even the best bed didn't stop one from feeling tight when they woke up. In a profession where a half second could be the difference between being dead and being paid, he didn't want a neck twinge screwing him over.

Limber and as relaxed as he ever allowed himself to get, Damian padded out to the kitchen wearing nothing but his boxers. There wasn't anyone to show off for; the last time he'd had a woman was more than a year ago, and he'd had her in a hotel and left a tip on the dresser. He just didn't like getting dressed before he had a shower, and he only had a shower before he had his coffee when shit was going down in a big way.

Shit was not going down in any kind of way just now. It was starting to get worrying, and Damian was starting to suspect what had happened.

Six months ago, his sister had fallen on hard times. Damian had distanced himself from his family as he fell deeper into the life, but he kept tabs on his baby sister. She'd gotten a frightening diagnosis, but her health insurance had started denying claims. He'd paid the tab anonymously, and now she was cancer free. Life was good.

But he hadn't had that kind of money just lying around. He'd gone to his contact with the Santiagos, the family with whom he did most of his work. He asked for a deal, a certain number of contracts in exchange for the money he needed to make sure his sister could keep her house. The contact had been happy to say yes. Damian had planned to either make his way on income from other jobs or pay back the Santiagos early.

But there hadn't been other jobs. You couldn't exactly list your services on Craigslist when you were a killer for hire, even when you moonlighted as a bodyguard. He could have burned one of his IDs to get a job in private security, but it seemed... ridiculous.

But what was more ridiculous was how the number of jobs he had to take—in order to pay off his debt—kept changing. The son of a bitch who he'd worked with kept saying he was "collecting interest." Damian was more and more confident that Todd Baker had no idea either what he was talking about or who he was dealing with—but he hadn't been able to suss out for sure whether or not Todd's stepfather, Carlos Santiago, actually did know what was happening.

Challenging Carlos on a debt owed was a good way to find himself in the ground. But being squeezed by Todd was getting old as well. Damian had more than a little money socked away and could easily live for the rest of his life without worrying, but there was more to it than the money. When he was still for too long, his body started to get restless. All the workouts and healthy living and careful training in the world didn't matter; he just got restless.

He wasn't a sociopath or a psychopath. His urges didn't push him towards killing. Just towards moving. As a kid, he'd had to move so often, and being still and settled hadn't ever worked for him as an adult.

Maybe he needed a woman. Not a pro, the kind of girl you picked up at a bar, but the kind who was willing to go a few rounds. Maybe it would be worth learning her name for once. Maybe he could fuck this restless feeling out of him. It would be worth a try anyway.

He made his coffee and drank it, black. He went to the shower; his morning wood was still very present, and he jerked off in the shower, harsh and efficient. Like everything he did lately. A woman might be good. A soft woman, soft tits, soft hips, soft ass. The sort you could dig your fingers into and leave behind marks.

Just the thought made him hard again before he'd even fully wilted back down to soft, and this time he stroked slow, letting the water smooth the movements of his hands as he let himself visualize that pretty girl. Vulnerable but not weak, soft-bodied but iron-willed. She'd writhe under him, maybe even put up a good-natured fight. The 'I never said yes, and you can't prove I did,' sort. Bever saying yes, but absolutely never saying no, and coming so hard on his cock that he thought she would break it off.

He groaned a second release at the thought and felt some of the tension drain out of him as he finished, smoothing out the last of the orgasm with a few short strokes of his hand. Yes. A woman or a job. One or the other, by tonight. And then, when he was calmer, he'd go to Carlos and ask what the hell was going on.

If Carlos had sanctioned the deal, then Damian might have some hell to pay, but if he hadn't... Carlos would want to know that Todd was going around and using his name. Todd was a stepson, not a full-blooded son, and Carlos hadn't raised him. He'd just fallen for Todd's mother. As far as Damian knew, the woman was barely even aware of her husband's second business.

Out of the shower and dried off, Damian got dressed. Clean jeans, tailored to his slim hips and strong thighs, and a black button-down shirt. Stereotypical? Maybe. Also practical. He'd run a few errands, take care of a few things around town, and then he would get in touch with people who could get him a meeting with Carlos Santiago.

Before he so much as walked out the door, his phone rang. Not the standard phone he used as an everyday cell; the phone that came with a very specific phone number. You had to pay a lot of money to even get the number, and then dialing it—well, retainers generally started as soon as he picked up the phone.

Of course, only one asshole had been calling that number lately. But that didn't stop the thrill that ran through him at the thought of a job. He picked up the phone but didn't say a word. No need.

"It's me," Todd Baker said, the stupid fucking son of a bitch. Damian kept his groan and his fury entirely internal. "I have a job for you."

Of course Todd had a job for him; the only reason anyone called this number was because they had a job for him. *Stupid shit.*

"Tell me."

"There's a target. He needs to be eliminated. It's my stepfather calling for this."

There was something shady as hell about that. If Carlos was involved, why wasn't one of his official lieutenants calling? But it was another thing Damian didn't quite dare ask. If the stepson of the capo ranked pretty low on the totem pole of family power, the hired hitter ranked even fucking lower than that. You took the job, or you didn't take the job, but the only questions you asked were things like where and when.

"Who is the target?"

"Rich Chamberlain."

That surprised Damian so much that he almost dropped the phone. Rich Chamberlain was the city's Tony Stark, the kind of guy who had buckets of money and was using it to do good things in the world, instead of just sitting around and using it to wipe his ass and upgrade his private jet every other month. Being a good guy put him in direct opposition to most of what the Santiagos did in the city. The Santiagos were a classic crime family; they ran drugs, guns, women, gambling rings, loan sharking, debt collection, everything. They eliminated threats to their business interests with extreme prejudice. But not Rich Chamberlain. You couldn't take out Tony Stark, not really.

Except, apparently, when you decided you could.

"Carlos called for this?" Damian wanted to smack himself as soon as the words were out of his mouth.

There was no excuse for him asking that sort of question, even if he was sure he was either being set up or—no, almost certainly set up.

Todd didn't like the question, and his tone made that very clear. "Chamberlain has stepped over the line this time, and we've had enough. There's an opportunity, and you are going to take it. I'll send the packet over by messenger in two hours. You'll need to be ready to move by tomorrow afternoon."

No part of this smelled good. Why would someone be going after Chamberlain now? What was going on? And why the hell was he getting tapped after so much time on the shelf? It tasted like Damian was going to be dealing with his own set of problems while this went down. But there was no option to say no. And he had—he glanced at his watch—just over 24 hours to research. He'd see what he could find out in that time, and see if he needed to disappear himself. He wouldn't enjoy doing it, but he could if he had to.

"Alright," he said.

He disconnected the call before Todd had a chance to do it. It was small and petty, but it still felt damn good.

The messenger arrived two hours later on the dot. At least some things could be relied upon in this world. Damian sat down at his desk with the thick envelope and opened it up, then spread the paperwork out.

Much of the information matched what he'd found during his initial research: Chamberlain was connected, protected, and a solid guy. He didn't have financial vulnerabilities, he'd never borrowed a cent on the shady side of the financial world, and he'd never so much as blinked at rooting corruption out of his various businesses. There was no crack in his armor, no failure to protect himself, no situation where Chamberlain was really dirty but really hiding it well. The man was just plain good.

For the first time, Damian thought he might actually feel truly bad about killing someone.

Todd was right about one thing though; for the first time, there was an in on Chamberlain. His kid was getting married, and as some kind of victory lap honeymoon thing, he was taking the kid on a cruise through international waters. His security detail was going to be dramatically reduced, and killing him outside of the United States would diminish significantly the ability for his death to be prosecuted —and, for the first time, make his businesses vulnerable to attack. *Fascinating.*

Todd had somehow gotten two invitations for the cruise, and that was supposed to Damian's in. But it only took him a couple of seconds to realize that was the flaw in this plan. This sort of trip was going to end up being a long con; he wouldn't have an exit until the yacht was back on the dock, which meant he couldn't be suspicious in any way.

To truly blend in the way that he would need to, he couldn't stand out. He was already a six foot three muscle-bound guy who had been told more than once that his good looks would make a woman fall over faint. Showing up without the plus one specified on the invitation—when it was very clear that the plus one was "highly encouraged"—would be a problem. The theme of the honeymoon was long lasting love or some shit. Entertaining, given that Chamberlain's wife had died ten years back. Then again, he hadn't had a girlfriend in a decade.

How could a person be this fucking pure and have no enemies?

Damian ran quickly through the contacts he had, trying to think of someone he trusted enough to run a game like this with him and came up blank. *Fuck it.* He picked up his phone and dialed a number. Not Todd; he had no fucking use for that idiot right now. He called Carlos. He would have to ditch the phone afterward, but he'd stop in at the nearest Best Buy and get a new one before he moved on; there was a new model out anyway, and he loved fresh tech.

"I'm surprised to hear from you," Carlos said in place of hello.

"I was surprised by this job," Damian replied. "The target is unusual."

Carlos was silent for a moment, and then Damian heard a door close. "What's wrong?" His tone was measured and calm, just like it always was.

"Not wrong, exactly."

*Bullshit.* If Damian weren't as careful as he was, this would be the kind of thing that got him chained up. Of course, maybe that was Todd's goal.

"But the invitation has a plus one attached, and showing up without one looks like it'll be… problematic."

Carlos gave a sigh that sounded long-suffering to Damian, though he'd never dream of saying such a thing to the man directly. *Yeah,* Damian found himself doubting that Todd Baker had anything like the pull he thought he did.

"A moment," he said, and the call disconnected.

It was about ten minutes before the phone rang again.

"Meet Todd at the corner of Van Buren and 22$^{nd}$ an hour before you're meant to board the boat," Carlos said. "Your 'wife' will be waiting for you."

# 3

Between the two of them, Piper and Marissa had eaten three tubs of ice cream, endless takeout, drunk an absurd amount of wine, and watched more old movies. Piper had passed out on the couch at least once and woken up covered with a soft blanket. Marissa had called in sick to work to stay there with her.

But after three days, Piper was done wallowing. She was the one who had broken up with Todd after all; it was more than a little ridiculous that she be the person to be this upset. However, the hardest part of the breakup, the part she hadn't expected, was how she kept remembering the little details of how she and Todd had been together. How he'd never quite listened to anything she had to say, or how he'd always gotten so angry out of nowhere when she'd contradicted him one too many times. How he'd been slowly, gently, wearing down her personality into becoming the person he wanted, not the person she was.

She'd tried to think of who she would have called if Marissa hadn't been there for her, but all of her friends had become their friends. She'd never been the type to have a million girlfriends as it was, but the ones she'd had since college had all drifted away since she and Todd had gotten more serious. It hadn't been intentional, but the places they were going kept being couple oriented, and even though she'd tried to arrange dates for her friends, people hadn't been interested. It was just Marissa, after a while. And only because Marissa was too stubborn to let go.

It was a frightening thought—wondering where she would have gone if not for Marissa. Piper tried not to let the thought take root; it wasn't going to do her any good, and it wouldn't make her feel safer. She was away from him now; that was the thing that mattered most. She didn't ever have to be close to him again.

She and Marissa had been up late again, and it had been Piper's turn to tuck Marissa into bed. She'd been sober enough to toss herself into the guest bed, so she woke up a little less stiff and uncomfortable than she had been the previous night. She stretched hard, feeling... safe. Calm. Relaxed. More like herself than she had in a very long time.

She glanced into Marissa's room and saw that her best friend was still sound asleep and snoring lightly. Piper grinned; even in college, Marissa had taken forever to sleep off a night of drinking, and they had gone three nights in a row.

Piper was hungry, and she wasn't in the mood for leftovers—well, whatever was still in the fridge. Plus, her mouth tasted like stale alcohol, and she knew she hadn't had a shower in a couple of days.

*Okay. First things first.*

She stripped off the underwear and T-shirt she'd slept in, then stepped into the shower. Marissa's favorite luxury was her shower; the rest of her apartment was the basic sort of place one got in the city. But she'd spent a fortune renovating one tiny corner of her bathroom. The shower had a temperature control, an in-shower music speaker, and a gorgeous rainfall designed showerhead.

Piper set the water to a high temperature, took a second to comb out her hair while the shower warmed up, and then stepped into the spray. She was sweaty and dirty, but that wasn't the only thing that the shower was washing away. It was like years of Todd—grime had accumulated on her skin, and as she let the water spray down over her, that sluiced down and drained away as well.

There was a song in an old musical her mother had loved, about washing that man right out of her hair. For the first time, Piper understood where the sentiment came from. She was washing Todd off her, and she was going to do everything possible not to think of him again.

She scrubbed her skin, washed and conditioned her hair, and then stepped out of the shower to blow dry her hair. Marissa had completely different products than her—Marissa generally encouraged her thick, coarse hair to curl so that she could do it up in a gorgeous twist out, while Piper often went for a flat iron—but she found some basic leave-in that wouldn't flatten her hair too much, and would at least keep her loose waves from going all kinds of frizzy.

She poked her head into Marissa's room again; Marissa was sound asleep. Piper sighed. She wanted a real breakfast, something good and hearty and filling.

*That's doable,* she thought after a moment.

She snuck into the room, grabbed a pair of jeans and a clean T-shirt, and got dressed. Commando, but fine. She and Marissa were close enough to the same size that she could make it down to the local diner and back.

She grabbed her purse, then locked the door behind her. She sent Marissa a quick text to let her know where she was going and then tucked her phone into her back pocket. Marissa turned off notifications while she slept, so Piper knew she wasn't going to wake her friend. Although maybe she would bring back some muffins and coffee. They could start being grown-ups again. Maybe Piper would even go back to her own apartment—though she had to admit that the thought of being alone made her stomach tighten a little.

She'd never thought Todd was a bad guy, just a slightly clueless one. But she had also never imagined the way he'd looked with his hand drawn back. She didn't know what had stopped him from hitting her, but she had a sudden and frightening belief that it hadn't been a sense of right and wrong. It had been a realization that he wouldn't get away with it.

And that made her wonder—how many women had he hit before when he'd known he could get away with it?

*No.* No, she couldn't think of that. It wasn't fair to her. She would end up blaming herself for any girls that had come after her, or irrationally, the ones who might have come before. But Todd was the only one who was responsible for his actions.

She was focusing on that thought when a hand clamped over her mouth and pulled her off her feet so hard and fast that she didn't get a chance to scream. Her nose wasn't covered entirely, but the fleshy hand that was pressed over her made it hard enough to breathe that she had to focus on just inhaling and exhaling; whatever noise she tried to make was swallowed by the vehicle which was already speeding into traffic.

She gasped deep breaths, trying to understand what in the name of God had just happened—and then looked up and understood. It wasn't just an SUV that she'd been tossed into; it was one of those quasi-limo jobs, where the two rows of seats faced each other. Sitting directly across from her was Todd, and he was grinning like a son of a bitch. The thoughts she'd been having just a few minutes ago, about how he would go on to abuse other women when he could get away with it, ran through her head hard. Did he think he could get away with it now?

"You're going to be useful to me," he said, and it sounded like every serial killer line ever spoken.

She launched herself at him, ready to claw his eyes out. It probably wouldn't help her get away, but it would feel good. But before she even moved half a dozen inches, there was a big hand hauling her back. She looked, for the first time, at the man who had snatched her. He was huge, white, bald, and looked like he could snap her in two like a man going Taekwondo on a couple of innocent pine boards.

"Put that on," he said, gesturing towards a garment bag laid out next to her.

She glanced at it, glared, and crossed her arms.

He raised an eyebrow. "You can put it on yourself, or I can put it on you while you are subdued. It's up to you. My way is more fun."

She could glare all she wanted, but the gleam in his eye turned her stomach. She had no doubt he would hold her down and force her into—whatever he wanted. She wasn't going to give him the satisfaction. If that was the most she could do, well... then that was all there was.

She opened the bag and found a dress that was pretty enough and roughly her size. Not fancy, just a jersey material that flared at the hips, but certainly more than she might have bought on her own. In her own world, Piper was mostly a jeans and sweater kind of girl. Where the hell were they going that she needed a kind of dressy but not really dressy dress?

She had to pull off her T-shirt to get the dress on over her head, but she managed to leave her jeans on and then wriggle out of them. At least Todd didn't get to see that she wasn't wearing panties.

*Small victories.*

Once she was decent again, Piper pitched her jeans directly at Todd's face. "Happy now?"

"You can't imagine how much," he said and kept on with his leering.

She forced herself to settle back against the car's seat and wait. There might be a chance to get out of this… but it wasn't now.

# 4

By the time Todd's SUV pulled into the parking lot, Damian was starting to get nervous. Not that he allowed himself to show outward signs of his concern; he was just a man, waiting for his "wife" to arrive.

He smiled to himself, checking his phone once for the time. The boat was scheduled to leave in half an hour. A few other couples were milling about, but being the last ones on the boat—or God help him, being someone the boat had to wait for—was exactly the kind of attention he did not want to draw to himself.

That was why he was standing against the railing, using his considerable skills to look like he didn't have a care in the world. It wouldn't help him to stand out. Keeping the outward appearance of being a man waiting for his "wife" to show up meant keeping the internal sense of being that man. Otherwise, it would all fall apart.

So, at the sight of the vehicle, he allowed himself just a moment of relief, then let it show on his face and in his stride in a very particular way. After so much concern, his fake wife for the day had finally arrived.

*About time!*

He opened the door in the back of the car, already reaching out a hand to the woman he knew would be there.

He didn't expect anyone like the woman he saw.

It wasn't just that she was drop dead gorgeous. She was pretty like the girl next door, a kind of pretty that would age into distinguished. She had soft red hair, the kind that was a deep warm red instead of that bright fiery orange color that was sometimes treated like it was the same. It fell over her shoulders in long waves that caught his attention. She was pale, her skin a light beige tone, with dark freckles all over her nose and her forearms.

The cold part of his mind protested that she would look too striking against his own darker, tanned complexion, but that was a level of paranoia that even he was uncomfortable with.

She was wearing a pretty jersey dress that showed off her curves without making them look out of proportion. The dress flared at the hips and somehow made him think of dancing. The deep blue color set off the much lighter blue of her eyes.

But what struck him the most—and instantly sent a wave of concern through him—was that this girl was absolutely normal. Her eyes were too soft. Her mouth was set in a thin line like she was holding back utter terror. He'd expected a prostitute, or at least another girl from within the Santiago family, not some random girl. Had Todd grabbed her off the street?

Behind him, the boat sounded the horn signaling all passengers to board.

Damian looked at Todd, his eyebrows raised high. "What is this?"

Todd grinned, and if Damian had ever doubted that the man was straight up bad news, his doubts vanished.

"She's your wife for the trip, just like you asked for." Todd leaned over and gave the woman's breast a grope, then turned her sideways enough to slap her ass. The woman gave a weak little yip, and her eyes closed hard. "And she's going to give you absolutely anything you want during this trip. She knows what sort of hell is waiting for her when she gets back here if she doesn't."

The woman's head snapped towards Todd, her eyes wide again—back to fear. She had no poker face at all. *Holy shit.* This was going to blow up right in Damian's face. But at the same time, he hated Todd. He hated that guy like he hated parsnips. And he would do an awful lot to get a woman away from that son of a bitch.

"Come here," he said, holding out his hand.

He couldn't remember the last time he'd tried to look gentle or soft. He doubted he was pulling it off well, but hey, a guy couldn't be good at everything. She stared at him for a long moment, then glanced back at Todd. He suspected she was thinking something similar to what he was: the evil you didn't know, sometimes really was better than the evil you did.

She took his hand and let him help her out of the car. Her hand was shaking in his, but her eyes didn't leave his face once they'd settled there.

"Bags," he said to Todd.

It wasn't a question. If the son of a bitch hadn't thought to bring this poor girl clothes, Damian truly was going to murder him and fuck what the Santiagos would do about it.

Todd nodded. "Already on the boat; I'm not a fucking idiot."

That was up for debate, but Damian gave a quick nod.

"I want to see you kiss the fucking bride," Todd said, and there was such malice in his voice that the girl trembled harder.

Damian looked down at her, at the tears glistening in her eyes. It would be the fastest way to get them out of here and get on to the job. He made his very best movie star impression, tracing his hand down her cheek and then lifting her chin. She seemed surprised at the gentleness, and he wondered in the back of his mind when someone had last been kind to her.

He wasn't any goddamn good at kind, and this was about as much gentleness as he had in him. He pressed his lips down on hers and felt her try to push away. Something deep inside of him unleashed; pretty women didn't say no to him. His arm tightened around her waist, and he pulled her so hard against him that she whimpered into his mouth. His tongue pressed hard against her lips and pushed them open so that he could push into her. If they weren't in public, he would have mauled her breasts, twisting her nipples until she screamed. Lucky for her it wasn't an option. He was hard as steel in his pants, and he wanted to throw her back in the SUV and fuck her until she screamed, no matter what she thought about it.

But he wouldn't give Todd the satisfaction. He forced himself to keep the kiss passionate but sweet and then stepped back away from her, keeping his hand in hers. He didn't say a word to Todd as he led the girl to the boat.

It only occurred to him once they were up the gangplank and being shown to their cabin that he didn't know her name.

# 5

Piper put everything she had into staying outwardly calm. Inward calm wasn't going to happen; her heart was slamming against her ribs like a bird trying to escape a cage, and her throat was so tight that she was afraid she would choke.

The nameless man had kissed her, and she'd wanted more than anything to bite his questing tongue and slap him and run. But not all of her felt that way, as twisted as it might be to admit it. Part of her wanted to reach out, pull him back, and beg him to kiss her like that again—fierce, mean, harsh and unrelenting.

But she pushed that thought away. She couldn't let herself think about this man—this monster—as someone desirable. She had no idea what Todd had done to her, but she was completely sure that she was potentially in incredible danger. After all, she'd just been held at gunpoint. That wasn't exactly how a good day started.

As the man led her towards the gangplank onto the yacht, she let out a little titter. She swallowed it hard, but it wouldn't stay down. It turned into a giggle, and she could feel more of them, the panicked swirling of desperate fear turning into hysterical laughter.

The man turned to her, his cold eyes staring down into her face. "Hold it together until we put our things in our cabin, or I swear to God that I will make your life absolute hell."

It should have made the laughter even worse, and it certainly didn't help. She forced herself to swallow it down, pretending to be the kind of woman who would wear this dress. She didn't know where the hell Todd had gotten it; it fit her too well to be off the rack, but how in the world would he have had it fitted to her? The color was gorgeous too. She hated it; every single thread.

She held onto the hatred and let it drown out the fear while the man led her onto the boat, handed over their tickets, apologized for holding everyone up, and asked how long until the ceremony. They were told that it would be an hour from now—to give the guests a chance to freshen up—and a cabin boy would show them to their cabin.

Piper followed in a daze. Choking down the laughter had somehow taken away all the other feelings as well, and now she didn't know what to do with herself. As she and the man were walking through the narrow halls of the ship, she felt the distinctive motion of the boat as it set out from the docks. Her stomach twisted hard—and not from seasickness. She pressed the back of her hand hard against her mouth, forcing herself not to gag.

The cabin boy led them up a level and opened the door to what she was sure was a gorgeous cabin. Her stomach twisted again, and she knew this wasn't going to be controllable.

"I'm so sorry," she managed to say, interrupting the man as he pulled cash out of his pocket to tip the boy. "Please point me to the restroom."

The boy didn't blink at all, just pointed. She walked for two steps, then realized that she needed to run.

She found the bathroom, slammed the door shut behind her, and dropped to her knees in front of the toilet as bile rose in her throat. She was the kind of sick that burned all the way through her, heaving so hard that she was afraid she would never be able to breathe.

Somewhere in the middle, she started sobbing. She tried to stay quiet; she didn't know what the man was going to do to her, or what she was going to be to him. It was entirely possible that she'd just been sold into some kind of slavery.

And there was a tiny, dark corner of herself that was deeply fascinated by it.

She was sick again, vomiting until there was nothing left to bring up. She flushed the toilet and leaned back, resting her head on the cool tile on the side of the bathroom. She was shaking, and she wrapped her arms tight around her knees, trying to pull herself into the smallest ball imaginable. She wanted to call Marissa and ask for yet another rescue—but her cell phone was in the pocket of her jeans, which were in Todd's SUV.

After a little while, the bathroom door opened. Piper thought about telling the man to learn to knock, but what was the point? She was his captive, apparently.

"You okay?" He leaned against the door jamb, watching her skeptically.

"Do I look okay?" No one said she had to be a polite captive.

It didn't seem to make him any angrier or more pleasant to have her sass; his face was so neutral that she wondered how long he'd practiced the look.

"No," he said. "And I need you to be okay."

"Then let me go back."

He put on a smile like putting on a shirt; there was nothing real about it.

"Can't make the boat turn around, and I need you here. Sorry. But when we get back to dry land, you'll be free to go, and I'll make sure that Todd pays you whatever he promised."

Piper blinked hard and fast. "He didn't—pay me."

The man's face seemed to darken for just a minute, and he brushed his fingers over his forehead for a moment, hiding his expression.

"Jesus Christ," he muttered. "Did that son of a bitch just grab you off the street?"

Piper laughed a little. "He actually did, the fucker. But we have history."

The man made a gesture to continue, and Piper sighed.

"We were dating. He was about to propose when I broke it off."

"That crazy fuck," the man said, almost to himself. He shook his head hard and looked up again. "Okay. So here's the thing. My name's Damian. I'm here to do a job. To get the job done, I need you here. You're camouflage. That's all. Just blend in, say the things I ask you to say, be Fiona's friend."

"Fiona?"

"The bride. There may be times when I need her out of the way so I can get the job done. Just—be prepared to go for a mani-pedi or something."

"What the hell kind of job do you do?"

His face went stone cold again, and Piper shuddered.

"Don't worry about that. What's your name?"

She thought for a moment about making something up, but what was the point of that. "Piper."

"Pleased to meet you. Let's get ready for a party."

He walked out of the room like this was a sane thing for two people to be doing, but at least it left her alone in the bathroom. She let herself shake for just a minute longer, and then pulled herself together. She didn't know what was going on, but she was going to have to go along with whatever it was to eventually get out of this.

Damian didn't seem like an actively bad guy—just a guy who had a job to do. Though it seemed obvious that whatever job it was, it was sinister. But still, there were lots of reasons that someone might need a fake wife. Such as a whole bunch of different cons, like on that one TV show she loved or getting a promotion from a boss who wanted to hire a family man. She could imagine the reasons but couldn't imagine someone who was working off of one of those reasons having such cold eyes.

That didn't matter. Right now, she needed to fix her makeup, brush her teeth, and get ready, apparently, for a party.

# 6

Damian kept his composure while he was in the bathroom with Piper, but once he was out, he couldn't keep the calm expression he'd schooled onto his face. Whatever "history" she had with Todd, it seemed obvious that he'd done this to her as some kind of punishment. That seemed in character with the vindictive asshole's previous behavior.

*No doubt—he is the dick to end all dicks.*

Damian wanted nothing more than to call Todd and explain to him, in lurid detail, why everything he'd done was wrong. Better yet, rat him out to Carlos.

Not for the first time in his life, he regretted ever borrowing money from the family. He was starting to wonder if he would get out of this before he died. It wasn't that he'd go and live some honest life or some kind of horseshit; he was a mercenary and had been for a very long time. He didn't mind that piece at all. He'd surveilled, he'd captured, he'd conned, and yes, he'd killed; none of it gave him nightmares. Maybe that meant, somewhere deep down, that he wasn't right in the head. He could only bring himself to care so much. This was who he was. And that was fine. He didn't need other things.

But the girl in that bathroom was innocent. Punishing her for breaking it off with him was stupid and cowardly, but he could understand how an asshole might feel like it was the only course of action to redeem his pride or some stupid shit. However, throwing her into a situation like this, both putting her in the line of fire and possibly causing the failure of the mission?

There was a cold part of Damian—the broken part, he figured—that briefly considered tossing her over the side of the boat. If she was going to die from being a part of this, better to get it over with sooner. He wouldn't be able to protect her from the things he was going to need to do to eliminate the target, and if she couldn't act like he was going to need her to act, then they were both going to end up arrested, at best, and dead at worst.

The ship was traveling into international waters. What was and was not a crime was very murky once you were outside of a country's borders. It meant that if someone realized he was the one who had taken out Chamberlain, it would be much harder for that to be prosecuted. It also meant that Chamberlain's private security force wouldn't have much trouble shooting Damian and disposing of his body. Out there, in the middle of the cold ocean, his body wouldn't even be found.

He wasn't a stranger to the reality of death or even the thought that he might be flirting with his own demise. The idea of his body sinking into those cold waters—unless he was buoyed by decomposition—filled him with a level of unanticipated dread.

He was going to get through this. After this, if Todd kept trying to hold his debts over his head, he was going to disappear. He was better at vanishing than Todd, or the Santiagos were at finding people. He would disappear. He could live a very comfortable life based off of the various funds he'd established in different countries where money couldn't be monitored well. Swiss bank accounts, money in the Caymans; more recently, transactions had happened in cyber currency, which was designed to be invisible and untraceable.

If that bubble ever burst, he would lose a significant chunk of his retirement fund, but that was why he diversified. And didn't throw out hard drives, like that one idiot. And in his estate planning was the password, in case his sister ever needed it. Invisible money was no good to anyone if you couldn't actually get it.

If the girl in the bathroom were useful, maybe he would even try to help her out. He'd see what happened. Either way, this was the last time he was operating as Todd Baker's personal wetworks man. Enough was enough. He'd done three times the contracts they'd agreed would pay off his debt; that was enough interest even for a mob family.

Then, there was the second thing that was frustrating him. He'd woken up that other morning, wanting a job or a girl. He'd gotten the job, in a way, and he'd put aside the longing for a girl. But kissing Piper early had reawakened the lust he'd put aside, big and fast. His cock was half hard in his slacks, and he was distracted by how very badly he wanted to fuck the girl. Jerking off wasn't going to be enough, not like this. He was one more kiss—or one finger buried in her wet cunt—away from being so throbbing hard that he would struggle to be sated.

He looked back at the bathroom and made a choice. If he was nice to this girl, she might think that she had a choice when he told her what to do. Better to make it clear from the beginning that he would tolerate no disobedience.

The bathroom door opened; she came out smelling of toothpaste. Her eyes were red-rimmed, but she was more composed.

"Did our luggage come?" she asked. "I assume Todd put makeup in there, hopefully, the stuff I'd left at his place—"

Damian moved lightning fast, burying his hand in the hair at the nape of her neck and snarling.

"I don't think I was clear enough in there," he said, making sure his eyes were as cold and hard as he knew how to make them. "This isn't a vacation for you. This isn't you having fun with your girlfriends. This is you, doing exactly what I say, whenever I say it."

He backed her up until she was pressed against the wall. Her palms were flat against the wallpaper, and her eyes were wide. His free hand took her breast in a tight grip. She was wearing a bra because he felt the strap when he ran his thumb over the circle. It was a thin one though, not one of those molded bras that stood up on their own. That meant that when he dug his fingers into the flesh of her breast, he felt the sink of his fingers in the tissue.

She cried out and squirmed; he let the weight of his body fall on her, pinning her to the wall. At the same time, he felt the small bud of her nipple tightening against his palm. She had reacted strongly when he'd kissed her harshly in the parking lot. Maybe she liked things a little rough.

Well, that just gave him license to be even more brutal.

"You're going to be my personal whore for the next month, do you understand? You're going to give me what I want, whenever I want it, and if I hear so much as a 'but' from you, then I'm going to whip your ass black and blue with my belt. If that doesn't convince you to behave, it'll be your tits next. Do you understand?"

She nodded as best as she could with her hair gripped the way it was.

"Say it."

"Y-yes." She moved against him, but he didn't think she was trying to get away.

"You little slut," he said, laughing to himself a little. "You like being told what to do, don't you?"

Her eyes darted to the side, and she didn't answer. He let go of her breast and slapped her, hard enough to sting, though not so much that he would leave a mark on her pretty face.

"Answer me, whore."

"Yes," she said again, with a little more confidence.

A pause, and then a mean little smile crossed her face.

"It's why I couldn't take Todd anymore. He wouldn't... take charge in the bedroom."

He read a world of meaning in those words, and he enjoyed it for a moment. He thought of reaching down to her cunt, dipping his fingers in her and making her taste just how wet he knew she was. But no, that wasn't what he wanted right now.

"Knees," he said, pushing with his hand as he took a step back from her.

Visible fear slipped back into her eyes again, but she knelt. His cock was achingly hard, and he worked his belt and his zipper without any hesitation. When he sprang free, her eyes went wider. He knew he was a big man, and he absolutely loved that moment when a woman looked at his dick and wondered, just for a second, how she was going to manage to take it.

Piper wasn't any different, and it made him even harder.

He didn't give her time to adjust, or plan, or anything like that.

He grabbed a fistful of her hair and warned her: "I better not feel your fucking teeth."

He steadied himself with one hand and pushed her down onto him with the other.

The warmth of her mouth surrounded him, and he groaned, biting back a curse. It had been too long since he'd fucked, too long since he'd been fucked. He had plenty of control, so he was nowhere near the edge, but he didn't want to bother with control right now. Part of him was tempted by the idea of spurting in her mouth almost right away, getting that initial release, and then letting her see that he was still hard before he shoved her back up against the wall and fucked her. To be gentle, he would only take her cunt and not her ass.

*No. No, not this time.*

This time, he was going to make it last, so she would understand what she was going to be giving him. What she was going to do, in exchange for him keeping her safe. Because if he were on edge all the time, it would fuck both of them over; better to fuck her and enjoy himself.

He groaned and thrust hard into her mouth, almost throwing her off balance before she steadied herself on her thighs. She was sucking him too gently, and it wasn't enough. He used his fist in her hair to push her down as he shoved himself into her mouth. Her eyes were big and wide, and he saw tears forming in them, but he didn't care.

When he felt the back of her throat, he pushed harder. The way she'd whimpered with pleasure when he shoved her up against the wall before showed him that she was the kind of bitch who could take it, and happily. Or, at least, could take it. Her eyes went even wider, and then she felt him swallow, and every goddamn inch of him was slammed into her mouth, her lips all the way down to the very base of his cock.

That was enough to almost make him lose control. He couldn't remember the last time he'd had his cock all the way down someone's fucking throat.

And it flipped some switch for her too. She'd been hesitant before, sucking him like a woman being forced into something she didn't really want. He knew better, he could see in her eyes how much the fear was turning her on. But after that moment, after having his whole cock buried in her, she began to suck him more eagerly. She moaned, her lips moving up and down his shaft, her hand at the base, tight and giving little strokes so that when she didn't take him quite as deeply, he was still wrapped up in her.

Fuck, he loved that. He put a hand on the wall to brace himself, but he didn't let go of her hair; there was no way he was letting her slow down, not when she was doing so well.

"Hungry slut." He hissed, and the tears that had been glistening in her eyes spilled over—but she sucked him twice as hard.

He felt his balls tightening, and he clenched hard, holding off his release and enjoying her work for another moment—until the pressure of the impending orgasm made his vision start to blur. He yanked her off for one moment, enjoying her squeak of surprise.

"I'm going to come," he said, "and you're going to swallow every drop. Hear me, bitch? If you spit a single dribble, I will gag your mouth so I can whip you until you're screaming. Do you understand?"

"Yes," she whimpered, and she was shifting on her knees like she was desperate for just a little pressure on her clit so she could get off too.

*No...*

No, a girl like her was dreaming that his big thick cock was buried inside of her.

He didn't hold back for another second, just shoved his cock back inside her mouth and thrust twice as hard.

# 7

Piper fought back the tears as Damian stuffed his enormous cock into her mouth again. She'd never dated anyone so big and had never tried to suck anyone half so huge. She hadn't thought cocks this big, ones she could barely fit her hand around, were real outside of porn. When he'd pushed past the back of her mouth into her throat, she'd thought she was going to choke on him—but it was making her so wet that she didn't care.

She was furious with her body for how she was reacting. He was forcing her into something she knew she didn't want, and her body was boiling hot, desperate for release in a way that she'd never felt before. Sex had always been something she endured, believing that it could be better, should be better, without ever knowing how to make it better.

But as he shoved into her mouth over and over, making her sloppy and slurping with her blow job, instead of the neat little things she'd learned to do with men who had smaller cocks, she was desperate to sneak a finger between her legs and rub her clit. She doubted it would take much to push her over the edge.

How was she so close to coming when she wished desperately that she was anywhere else?

When he pulled back, told her that she was going to swallow every drop of his cum, she forced herself to stay quiet, other than her whisper of yes. He didn't wait, just pushed back into her. She felt how much more swollen he was, and with her hands on his thighs, she felt the big muscles there tightening as he prepared to let himself go. She wanted to shake her head, try and fight back, but he would just hold her down harder, and she'd have to take it anyway. This way, at least, she could keep from drowning.

The only warning she got from him was a long, thick groan, and then he was spasming inside her mouth, rush after rush of hot cum, so fast she could barely swallow. She did though—forced herself to do what he'd demanded of her—and keeping her hand moving slowly around the base of his cock, gave him that last bit of pleasure.

Even if she was being forced into something she didn't want, she was going to make sure she did it well.

He staggered for a moment, the grip on her hair loosening a little. His eyes were unfocused as he gazed down. Then he blinked, pulled free from her mouth, and gave her a light slap on the face.

"Good fucking girl," he said. "Don't forget that you didn't fight back."

His hand tightened in her hair again, and he pulled her to her feet. He shoved her until her back was against the wall, and then his hands dug under her skirt. His hand moved away from her hair so that he could grope her breast, digging in his fingers and pinching at her nipple.

When his fingers found the elastic of her panties, fear slammed through her. Being shoved down on his cock to give him a messy blow job was one thing; this was another. His weight held her in place, and he was so much bigger than her that there was no chance of dislodging him—but that didn't stop her from trying.

She arched her back, trying to get enough leverage to shift the weight on her upper torso, where he'd focused it. But that just pushed her hips closer to his questing fingers. He slipped her panties to the side, as if they weren't even there, and stroked her cunt with two fingers.

She went wild, pushing at him with her hands, bucking her hips harder, pulling away from him, trying anything she could to get free. It was like shoving at a granite statue—and he hadn't done up his pants. She saw his cock swelling again as she fought. He wasn't— could he be hard again so soon? And if he could, what was that going to mean for her. She had a flash of how much it would hurt to take such a big, fat cock, and she found herself fighting even harder. She opened her mouth to scream, and then he slapped her again.

"Don't make a goddamn sound, you hear me?" His voice was calm and quiet in her ear.

She went still. This wasn't something that she was going to get out of —and what that meant, if she couldn't.

His fingers were on her lips, and he shoved them into her mouth, just like he'd done with his cock. She hadn't thought of biting then, but she thought of it now. However, the fierce look in his eyes kept her from doing it. She had seen how cold he was before. She doubted that he would even think twice before... well, doing something horrible to her—she didn't know what.

"Suck," he commanded, and she did before she wondered if she should.

His fingers tasted—spicy, tangy, warm, and wet as hell. She realized what was happening just before he said it.

"That's how dripping wet your cunt is. Don't fucking pretend you don't want this." He pulled back and grinned, though the expression didn't warm up his eyes at all. "If you're fighting because it turns you on, then, by all means, keep going. I love a girl who fights. But if you actually think you're going to get away?"

Another slap.

"I told you. I need you here to do my job. And I will do what I need to do to make sure that it gets done. If that means drugging you throughout this, I'll do it. If that means fucking you into submission every night, I'll do that too." The grin got a little wider. "Actually, that sounds fun. You want to know that you're getting fucked every night, whether you want it or not, Piper?"

Something about the way he said her name twisted the fear into something... *darker* and *hungrie*r. She whimpered a little.

"I see," he said. "I like a girl who knows what she wants. And you're a pretty girl. I'll enjoy taking what you have to give. No matter how much you like me taking it."

And then his mouth was on hers, and his fingers were stroking her pussy through her panties again. She felt herself gushing, wanting so much more of this. His forcefulness, his pushing her to accept whatever he thought was best—it was turning her on until she was humping against his hand, hoping for a little more pressure on her clit.

He stroked a single finger through her folds again, then pushed two inside of her. The stretch was shocking, but she was so sopping wet that it wasn't hard for him to push them in deep, then drag them out with a little twisting motion that had her whining against his hard mouth. When he added a third, though, she felt stretched almost to the point of pain. She tried to pull away again, but his hand followed her, and he started thrusting harder as she started to cry again.

"My cock is bigger than this," he said, whispering in her ear again. "And you're going to take that. You're going to come on my cock, no matter how much you hate it, no matter how much you try to fight, because I want it. Do you understand?"

Piper shook her head, hard. His fingers, forcing their way into her cunt, spreading and twisting, stretching her past where it hurt—she didn't want this. She didn't. She didn't want to be fucked this way—there was a darker word for it—and the pleasure was gone; she was sure she couldn't have come, no matter how he tried to work for her pleasure.

Except she did want this. Somewhere in her head, she did want this, to be treated like this, because she was still gushing on his hand, soaking him, and she felt pleasure swirling through her, eager and desperate and unlike anything she'd ever experienced.

He didn't slap her this time, which surprised her. Instead, he just made a sad clucking sound of disappointment.

"Shame. If you'd been a good girl, I would have fucked you like a pretty thing. Instead?" He looked around.

There wasn't much in the cabin, even though she was pretty sure it was a luxury cabin. It was the size of a smallish hotel suite, which seemed pretty fancy for a boat.

He pulled his hand free. Her cunt made the most disgusting squelching sound as he did, but she didn't have time to worry about it. He shoved her over to the bed, and she fell on it. She started to roll over onto her back, but he flipped up her skirt and gave her ass a huge slap. She cried out for the first time, then crammed her own fist into her mouth. He'd said to be quiet, not to make a sound. She had to—if she didn't do what he said, she didn't know what would happen.

"You stay where I put you," he said.

She did, her torso lying on the bed, her feet on the floor. The slap on her ass stung like a thousand tiny needle pricks. She could imagine his handprint there, bright red, where anyone could see it. Evidence of what had been done to her. What she'd accepted.

He took the pillows from the head of the bed, made a little pile at the foot of it, then picked her up again by her hair and shoved her down, her hips raised up by the pillows. She heard his jeans hit the floor and felt him pull her underwear down past her knees.

"There," he said, and those three fingers plunged into her again.

There was more room for him to move now, and as he spiraled them inside of her, she felt that hot pleasure twist through her again, making her gasp and push back against his hand.

He slapped her ass again, and she turned her face into the mattress to muffle the cry.

"You're not fighting to get away now, are you?"

Another slap.

"I think you want me to fuck you. I don't think it matters how much you protest. I think you want my cock."

She was searing hot, and she wanted him, even if the shame of it made her cheeks burn. She nodded, hesitant, at first, and then harder.

"Say it," he said, his fingers twisting harder and faster.

At this speed, his thumb bumped into her clit with every stroke, and she wanted the release of an orgasm more than ever. Somehow, that would make this whole thing... more tolerable. She could live with whatever came next, somehow, if she was coming on his cock, harsh and vicious and like she'd always dreamed.

Another harsh slap to her ass.

"I said say it."

Piper groaned long and low and then forced herself to speak. "I want it."

He slapped her again, the same spot. She felt it burning, searing into her flesh. She would never forget the sensation.

"What do you want?"

His fingers pulled free with another of those long, wet sounds, and she was horribly empty. They were replaced by what felt like the head of his cock, but when she tried to push back eagerly, he just spanked her again.

"Your cock." She gasped, needing desperately to be full. "I want your cock."

He gave it to her in one swift motion. He had opened her up so wide that it was nothing for him to fill her up, pressing deep inside of her with a long, hard rush. He let out a groan as he bottomed out in her, and she felt his hips against her ass.

Every long, thick inch of him fit inside of her, and even as she was stretching even more to accommodate his incredible girth, she felt her body surging around him, squeezing, desperately close to the edge even though he'd barely started fucking her.

From the way he was moving, with jagged, sharp bursts, she was sure he was as tight and close as she was. He grunted at the end of each thrust, moving his hips in some magical way that was making her clench her fists in the sheets and twist them, trying to keep control of herself. This was humiliating, terrifying—and she'd never been so turned on in her life.

"You like it, don't you," he said, his voice rough and breathless. "You like not having a choice. You like that you're trying not to come around my thick cock when you're taking it by force."

He didn't like it when she was quiet; she'd figured out that much.

"Yes," she cried out.

"You're going to come like a whore, aren't you? A pretty whore who's already thinking about how this is going to be her life for as long as I choose for it to be, and wondering if she got the good end of the deal."

"Yes."

God, she was trying to hold back, and she didn't know why. It felt good, it felt incredible to be pushed into this—she would be ashamed of it later, but she wasn't ashamed of it now. Now she was desperate to let go, and she wasn't sure how much longer she could hold on.

She felt him slam into her one last time with a groan, and that thumb that had been teasing her clit clamped down, twisting the sensitive nub until she was burying her face in the mattress to hide the scream. Pleasure screamed through her as she felt his cock pulsing, throbbing inside of her as he came.

Everything twisted down into one tiny pinpoint of sensation and then burst through her, making her hips shove wildly back at him, rocking on his still spurting cock. He was so big and thick that she felt their mixed fluids leaking out onto her thighs as he rode out those last few strokes with her, urging her through every bit of pleasure she could take from it. Her body was entirely limp and boneless, and she had to work to turn her head sideways so she could breathe.

*Condom*, she thought distantly. *Oh shit.*

But would he have really stopped if she had demanded that he put one on? She certainly didn't think so. And right this second, she couldn't muster up the energy to care. Timing wise, she should be fine. Probably.

*Girl. Least of your concerns. Focus.*

He had backed up now, his gorgeous cock slowly becoming flaccid, though even soft he was absolutely huge. Piper rolled sideways. She was incredibly messy, and she didn't want to mess up the dress she was in—not until she knew if she actually had other clothes anyway.

But that was tomorrow's problem.

Damian ducked through a door, then came back out with a couple of towels in hand. He tossed one to Piper, and she found her cheeks flaring red as she used the softest towel she'd ever touched to wipe up a mix of cum and arousal that would have looked excessive in a lot of porn.

Damian's face was calmer now. When Piper had cleaned herself up and sat up—taking a moment to really feel how it burned to have the ass cheek he'd spanked so many times take her weight—he sat down next to her.

"I think we both needed that," he said, using the same voice a person might use to comment on the weather.

It was too much to admit that she had enjoyed herself; she definitely was not about to say that she'd needed something so rough and brutal. With her body covered and theoretically decent again—although her panties were so soaked and filthy that she really just wanted to take them off and go without—it was harder to understand why it had felt good. Why being forced to take something like that had felt so freeing.

She was just going to put it in the past and find out what she needed to do to survive—whatever it was that was happening—the next month on this yacht.

# 8

Damian resisted the urge to rub his eyes. This girl wasn't going to be useful in any of the ways he needed her to be. Well, his cock ached from the fury with which they'd fucked, and he was still so turned on that he was sure he could take her again tonight—if he decided he wanted to. But other than that, he had to admit that there was something particularly enjoyable about taking the girl who had rejected Todd; son of a bitch had it coming. He would bet his entire retirement money that she'd never screamed like that for Todd.

What he had needed was a piece of arm candy, a girl who could be friendly enough with the bride and not be in the way when he needed to get things done. He did not need an amateur Nancy Drew asking questions or drawing conclusions, or really doing anything other than "what he said to do". It was something simple.

But she wasn't going to make it simple as she had just asked about the job.

"No, I won't tell you what the job is," he said, making his voice hard and clear. "And if you ask me again, I'm going to show you the difference between a fun spanking and one that I mean. Clear?"

Her eyes went big before she blinked and got herself back under control. Interesting. Prim little darling had no idea how much she liked the pain. He could use that—if he needed to.

"Okay," she said. She seemed scared. That was okay. Frankly, given the day that she'd had, she should be scared. "Can you tell me more clearly what you need me to do?"

"No," he said again, then held up a hand when she started to argue. "It's going to be a work in progress. I can give you a little bit of background here—and you need to fix your makeup. We need to multi-task, or we're going to be late."

He dug through the bags that Todd had sent onto the ship for them. Eventually, Piper made an "Ooh!" sort of sound, and he handed her the bag his hands were on. She opened it up and made a face; apparently, it was a bunch of leftovers from what she'd left at Todd's condo. Well, it would do, and if it wouldn't, the ship would have some sort of make-up counter; he was sure of that much. She stood, wobbled on her feet for a moment, then went into the bathroom.

"This is a wedding cruise," he said. "We're here to wish Fiona Chamberlain and her fiancé, Alex Dodson, well as they embark on their next stage of life. Embark, like a ship, I guess. The theme connection is unclear."

Damian made himself pause and recollect. Watching her wash off the makeup that he'd ruined fucking her was incredibly distracting. As she reapplied it fresh, all he wanted to do was ruin it again.

This had the potential to become a real problem.

"It's Fiona's father, Rich, who I have business with. To be able to deal with him, I need to deal with Fiona, and that means getting close to Fiona. That's going to be your job."

Piper nodded as she carefully applied eyeliner. "So I need to be friends with the rich girl getting married? Okay."

Damian shook his head. "It's a tiny bit more complicated than that. You and Fiona are already friends; you have been for about ten years now."

Piper blinked, messed up the eyeliner, cursed, and then set about fixing it. "I don't know anyone named Fiona."

He resisted the urge to roll his eyes. "Fiona was apparently quite the party girl for a while in college. She had a suite with girls moving in and out frequently for a few weeks. She invited absolutely everyone from those days to join her here, and that means you're here. You lived in the suite for about three weeks before you transferred out to another school. Except for that detail, all the rest of your story stays yours."

"There's not some kind of complicated backstory I have to memorize?"

This was going to be a fucking disaster, and he was going to hang Todd by his balls for this. If Damian survived it.

"No. You always keep your story as simple as possible. The less complicated it is, the easier it is to remember, and the harder it is to fuck up. And that's basically your job here—be friends with Fiona, don't fuck up. Think you can handle that?"

He saw Piper bristle, her eyes narrowing for a moment. It looked damn sexy, and he wanted to make her do it again. Just for fun.

"While juggling," she said. "Where are we going now?"

"There's a short reception beforehand, then the wedding, then a full reception after." Damian glanced down at his watch. "We're just fashionably late for the early reception, but if we don't get a move on, we'll actually be late." He looked her up and down. The dress that Todd had shoved on her did look good, and it wasn't too wrinkled after everything he'd done to her. There was just one detail… "Give me your panties."

"Excuse me?" She almost stabbed herself in the eye again, with a mascara wand this time, but she recovered at the last moment. "Do what?"

"They're soaking wet, and they're making you fidget. Take them off. You can go without, you'll be fine."

Her cheeks flared as red as if he'd slapped her, and goddammit just thinking that was making his dick hard again. He clenched down hard, forcing himself to keep the blood from flowing into that area. He didn't have time to be a fucking teenage boy nutting off every other minute.

"They're not wet." She lifted her chin in a saucy, defiant little way that made him furious and made all the clenching in the world irrelevant. His dick sprang to full attention, completely uncaring that it had been well tended to just a few minutes before.

He shoved her again, loving the squeak she made to find herself pressed up against a wall with his weight bearing down on her.

"I think you forget," he said, lifting her skirt slowly as she tried and failed to wriggle away.

He dug his fingers into her fleshy thigh hard enough to make her hiss and be still. He pressed his fingers over the crotch of her panties, feeling the cold wetness there and shoving it up against her. She made a face and squirmed harder, clearly disliking the sensation. Of course she did; no one would want to be sitting around in dirty underwear—unless that was their kink, in which case, respect.

"You're forgetting who made them wet in the first place." He caught the edge of the fabric and snapped it sharply against her skin once, then started to tug them down.

It was hard; they caught on the curves of her hips and thighs, but she had the sense not to try and press her knees together. He got them down and off her feet, then checked. She hadn't done her lipstick yet; he smeared the filthy panties over her mouth. She tried to twist away, and he grabbed the back of her head, holding her still so that he could shove them against her lips.

"Don't forget."

Her eyes were wide, and she shook her head. He considered making her say it just so he could cram the panties in her mouth. But no. They had places to be.

He pulled the panties back and raised an eyebrow.

"I'm sorry," she said. "I won't... forget."

He stepped back and enjoyed how her hands were shaking as she washed her chin and lips and then finished off her makeup.

# 9

When she walked into the ballroom on Damian's arm, Piper couldn't believe what an opulent space she had entered. She'd been to black tie events once or twice, either through her career or with dates, but this was something that gave a new definition to the concept of excess. It reminded her of the old photos of the Titanic, all gilt and red carpet and glittering glass.

There were a few chairs set around the outside of the room, a few high tables and then regular tables and chairs organized on the far side of the room. Most of the space, however, was simply open, leaving space for guests to mingle. Waitstaff with white gloves moved through the space, circulating small plates and amuse-bouche and glasses of champagne and wine. There was a wet bar to the left.

Piper leaned towards Damian and turned her head so that anything she said would probably seem like a lover's whisper, even though the thought made her shudder a little. Not necessarily unpleasantly.

"Am I allowed to drink?"

He turned towards her, his mouth curved in an affectionate smile while his eyes studied her in an entirely different way. "Are you a sloppy drunk?"

She gave a light laugh that she hoped was what he was looking for in Fiona's future best friend.

"Absolutely not. I don't usually have more than a glass of wine or a single drink anyway, but I don't get messy that fast anyway."

He shot her a knowing look, and her cheeks flared red. In the bathroom, when he'd been so humiliating... it had twisted her up inside in a way she just didn't understand. It was like he was reading her mind and sneaking peeks at her darkest fantasies. It was terrifying—and arousing, both in ways that were difficult to all the way comprehend.

She wasn't sure she wanted to—if she was entirely honest. There were so many things she had buried far away when she'd realized that there wasn't a man she would ever be able to tell about them. The few times she had suggested things to college boyfriends, they'd been disgusted, horrified that she would even think of such things. So, she'd stopped—pretended that no one would want anything like that, and definitely not her.

No matter how much it was a lie.

"Fine," he said.

He snagged two glasses of dry white wine—*thank God*, she hated champagne—from a waiter as the tray went by.

"Have you had anything to eat yet?"

"No," she said.

It had been hours ago—or had it been?—since she'd left Marissa's apartment for breakfast.

"Then sip that slow, and find something to eat. I'll be over at the tables. We'll go up and greet Fiona and Alex together."

Piper nodded. While the staff was circulating with small things, there were also a few other plates laid out, buffet style, on a long, tiered table. She went over, selecting a few small things, and giving herself a moment to breathe while she thought about what the hell she was going to do to get out of this.

The fact that the sex she'd just had was life-changing, she had no idea what was going on here. Clearly, Damian was here to do something illegal, or else she wouldn't be here. Some kind of con or something that she absolutely did not want to be caught up in. But the boat was already in motion; even though they were on a huge ocean liner that was barely moved by the average wave, she felt the rumble of the engines beneath her. Jumping ship and swimming to shore was a romantic dream that would just end up with her drowned.

She could reveal herself to a crew member, but Damian and Todd were certainly involved in something together. It seemed more than possible that at least some of the crew had been bought. If she tried to leave, there was no guarantee that she would get away with it. And if she was a liability… Damian had implied that as long as things went the way he told her they should, he was going to do his best to protect her. Even make sure she got paid for "services rendered". It sounded a lot like getting paid to be his personal whore, but at least it was enjoyable.

But what if the—whatever—that he was involved in was deeper than just some kind of con, or maybe the kind of business deal best conducted outside of American oversight? What if he was here to do something really bad?

Piper looked back over her shoulder and saw that Damian was no longer where she had left him. Her heart skipped for a moment, but she pushed herself to remember:

*He said that he would meet me by the tables. I'll find him there in just a moment*—when she decided whether she was going there at all.

She ate two tiny meatballs off an artfully carved skewer, had one of the most sumptuous egg rolls she'd ever tried, and then made short work of a slice of chocolate mousse cake the length and width of a finger. She wanted to eat plenty more; once she'd swallowed one thing, it was like her stomach woke up and tried to scream its needs into her face. But if she overate too much, she would feel sick, and none of this was going to go well if that happened.

She looked to the tables, and saw Damian there, drinking his glass of wine and holding hers. She took one more long moment, trying to decide what to do, and walked back towards him. Without a clear plan, flailing around would just put them both in danger.

She didn't know if the crew was safe, and she didn't really know who this family was. Well, she knew who Rich Chamberlain was. His name was gold in the city's commerce centers. He was a billionaire, and he'd worked hard for his fortune. He seemed to be a genuinely good guy too—but then lots of men seemed decent right up until you put them into a corner. He must have had some kind of dealings with the Santiagos; that didn't mean anything good for him. This entire ship might be one big death trap for her.

Her heart slammed as she walked across the dance floor, smiling and weaving through people who were all trying to get close to one particular couple. *The happy bride and groom to be*, she assumed. She would meet Damian, she'd drink her wine, and they'd go pretend to know the couple. Hopefully, Fiona would accept the story. If not... then either Damian would find another way to make her useful, or he wouldn't. The thought of what could happen after that was terrifying.

So, she would simply need to make sure that her performance was absolutely perfect.

"Mr. Demille," she murmured as she got close to Damian and reached for her glass. "I'm ready for my close-up."

He smirked, lifting his glass in a toast. "I'm sure you are. Do you have questions?"

"Is there anything in particular you need me to say? To not say?"

He shook his head. "No. She's a nice kid, from what I understand, Good to her friends, volunteers at pet shelters, reads to kids in schools—if there's a calling card for a nice person, she's got it on her resume. As far as I can tell, too, she's just genuinely nice. It's not some trap to lure people into some snare. She's just a good person."

*There are worse things*, Piper thought.

"Do you know anything about what she likes? Personally, I mean?"

Damian shook his head. "I trust you to find out."

"Okay." She leaned up and gave him a kiss on the cheek, careful to keep it light enough that her lipstick wouldn't transfer. "Let's go see what's happening then."

Damian set down both of their glasses, then held out his elbow for her to take. She smiled and threaded her hand through. Her heart was slamming in her chest, but she forced herself to keep breathing.

*The only way out is through*, she reminded herself. *Become friends with the girl. That won't be hard.*

And it wouldn't be. Piper had always had an easy time making friends. She had a knack for keeping conversations just neutral enough to avoid offense until she knew what someone might like or not, and then she could dig in. She'd never yet found a topic she was bored by, not from infosec to the perfect winged liner creation. She loved new things and new learning. She would find something that she and Fiona Chamberlain could be passionate about together.

The crowd around the couple was thick, but Damian seemed to be a master at making space for his broad-shouldered frame to work its way through. He brought Piper with him without any noticeable effort, and the two of them were at the inner circle before Piper really got her bearings.

Fiona was absolutely radiant. She wasn't pretty, exactly, but she was so happy that she looked truly beautiful. She wore a big smile, her eyes were open wide, and happiness just seemed to shine out of her pores. In an old romantic movie, someone would have sighed and commented on young girls in love. She had pretty brown hair that had been styled into an updo and subtle makeup that enhanced her face like a movie star.

When they got close, Damian reached out and shook the groom-to-be's hand.

"Alex Goddamn Dodson, how are you?" he said, clapping Alex on the shoulder as they shook hands.

Piper tried not to look at him in total shock. Everything about the man was completely different. He wore a smile like a hat he'd put on, and his eyes twinkled with contained laughter.

What blew Piper's mind was the way Alex smiled back and shook Damian's hand with vigor. It was like they really did know each other.

"Hi! Yes, you're… in accounting—"

"Damian, yes," Damian said, and that grin got a little bigger. "When Rich said he was inviting everyone—all the department heads and subs—I didn't realize that he meant *all* of us. I'm just honored to be here with you guys."

Damian turned towards Fiona and reached out to shake her hand as well. The gesture was just a little different, subtler, but Fiona flashed him a big smile.

"And we couldn't believe it, could we, honey?" Alex said, the last bit directed towards Piper, who smiled and nodded eagerly. "At least, I couldn't believe that your fiancée and my wife had been roommates for a little while in college."

Fiona had dropped Damian's grip, and she turned to look at Piper a little more carefully. *Interesting.* It didn't feel like she was being studied by a party girl; it seemed like she was being measured up by a businesswoman. She had a kind of effervescent personality in her mind, a dialed-up version of who she was when she was a little overwhelmed but really happy. On instinct, she dropped that. Whoever had told Damian that Fiona was a party girl, Piper didn't believe she was the kind of girl who got blackout drunk and forgot who she lived with.

Piper reached out her hand.

Fiona took it, still watching her with the same, careful look.

"Hi," Piper said. "I don't blame you if you don't remember me—"

Fiona shook her head. "Oh, no, I do, I think. Sophomore year, right at the end of the spring semester. You took over Jackie's room for a month or so when she took off after spring break."

"Yes!" Piper grinned and found Fiona matching her smile. "Wow, after all this time."

"It's surprising," Fiona said, then pulled Piper in for a sudden hug. "But I'm really glad you're here."

The arms around her shoulders, the soft pressure—it felt surprisingly nice and reassuring. Something in Piper's head clicked over, and she realized that she'd never had sex with a new guy and not been able to debrief with Marissa immediately afterward. This girl wasn't Marissa, clearly, but man, being held like that felt nice. She squeezed back and just let herself be for the single moment of the embrace.

"I'm glad I'm here too," she said, and when she pulled back, she found Fiona wearing a grin that matched hers.

"I don't have a lot of time this second," Fiona said. "And I expect to be busy tonight." There was a long, scorching-hot look at her soon-to-be husband. "And maybe tomorrow."

*My oh my. Clearly not waiting for the wedding night.*

"But as soon as I can, I'll send someone by, okay?" Fiona added. "We've got everything on this boat. We can go for coffee, have a massage, go swimming. And the cruise plan takes us all over the Caribbean, and into some of the coastal South American countries. There'll be lots of chances to catch up. I can't wait to hear what you've been up to all these years. Okay?"

"Absolutely," Piper said.

She felt the gentle pressure of Damian's hand on her arm, and she let him take her to the side and give way to the next couple trying to catch the attention of the soon-to-be-married couple.

"That was too easy," he said, once they had retreated slightly. "You didn't actually go to college with her?"

"Nope," Piper said. "I went to a state school. That girl did not go to a state school."

"You have that right." Damian studied the couple.

It was interesting, watching him. Piper knew he was staring at them to try to pick out some small detail. She didn't know what it was, just that it was catching his attention and not letting go. But he didn't look like he was looking at them. She could track it, but she doubted it would be immediately obvious to anyone else.

Except for one man. As she let her eyes wander through the crowd, she saw one man staring in their direction, his gaze unblinking. She wanted to flinch and turn away; it was the sort of stare that made a person want to confess their sins and flee. He wasn't wearing a clerical collar or robes, though, so she didn't think he was any sort of priest. He was just a man who was accustomed to looking straight through people.

She forced her gaze to pass over him, hoping that he wouldn't have registered whatever subtle—or not so subtle—signs she might have given that she had noticed his attention. She didn't know what to do or how to do it; she wanted to somehow signal Damian that something was going on, but she didn't know how to get his attention without it being obvious.

So she looked over at the happy couple, and let herself see how happy they were. How much they were smiling, how they kept looking at each other. How they seemed to glow with it. She let that permeate her, and then she looked up at Damian. She let the lust from before flow through her again, running through her hard. She thought of him pushing her back against the wall, over and over, abusing her body and taking her against her will—but also how he'd gotten her wine and gently made sure she was alright after he'd taken her so harshly.

She let that same gushing heat that she saw between Fiona and Alex run through her, and she reached out and stroked her arm down his hand. When Damian glanced towards her, his eyebrows lifted, she leaned up, locked her arms around his neck, and pulled him down into a kiss.

She had expected something like the heated kiss on the docks, but hot damn. That had been an ice cream cone on a January day compared to this. He snarled into her mouth, his arm locking around her waist and one hand on the back of her neck before she could blink. He was shaking just a bit, and as he pulled her snug against her, she felt him, just as iron hard as before in his dress slacks.

A huge part of her wanted to drop to her knees and suck him off then and there, in front of God, and anyone else who wanted to look her way. She gave good blow jobs. Someone here could certainly take some tips. Someone would film it and put it on YouTube, and she would make a fortune.

*He's never going to stop wanting me.* The thought made wetness gush between her thighs. *He's never going to let me go.* Somehow, that thought was even harder. Forget blowing him. He could hike up her skirt and bend her over one of these fucking chairs, and she wouldn't say no.

He forced the kiss to a stop, both of them panting.

"What was that?" he asked, their foreheads still pressed together.

His mouth was bent in a grin, and his eyes were crinkling at the corners like he was smiling, but the actual look in his eyes was laser tight and focused.

"There's a man to our, um, to your nine? Right?"

He laughed, and that was genuine. At least a little. "On my right is fine."

"Okay. On your right. Tall, skinny, brownish hair. Gray suit. He was staring straight at us. Like, not just in our direction, right at us. Like he knew something was up."

Damian cursed, then leaned down and pressed another, lighter kiss against her lips. It didn't do anything to tamp down or extinguish the lusty fire searing through her. She forced herself to keep breathing and to try and stay calm. Stay calm enough so that she wasn't dripping halfway down her thighs.

"Stay here," he said. "I need to circle around a little."

Piper nodded and pulled herself up into a seat while Damian stepped away. He wandered towards the buffet table, saying hello and shaking hands every so often as he walked along. He was a gorgeous man, and personable—at least when he wasn't cold and cruel like he'd been in their cabin before. Which Damian was the real one?

Somehow, Piper doubted this would be the first time she would ask herself that question. Not for the first time she hated that she hadn't at least tried to get her phone out of her purse before Todd had tossed her out of the car. She could have called Marissa. The police. Hell, she could have played some Candy Crush while she waited for something to happen. She was really fucking bad at holding still.

But there was nothing else to do. At least, not right now.

## 10

There was no part of Damian that was calm right now, and the raging erection wasn't helping. He had some experience with hiding those, and he had plenty of experience with pretending that everything was fine when it was not even remotely fine. What he did not have much experience with was doing all of those things while also worrying about a civilian who had been roped into this nonsense with him.

The thing was—a prostitute would have stood out as a prostitute, and frankly, no one on the boat would have noticed. He'd spotted three working girls here being—he hoped—well paid and well treated in exchange for making it look like guys who spent this much time with their noses in their stock portfolios could attract women as gorgeous as that. At least a couple more were here on the opposite side of the coin—somehow getting an invite or an in and hoping to meet Daddy Warbucks on the cruise. And that was fine. Live and let live. He wished to hell that Todd had bought him a prostitute.

A family girl would have been a risk. The Santiagos leaned towards loud and obnoxious, not the kind of girls who would charm Fiona Chamberlain into friendship. And they were well known. The Santiagos had enough above board businesses the girls could lay claim to that they didn't take shame in dropping their parents' names around town. But that same visibility ran the risk of connecting him to the family—the exact thing he was trying to avoid doing.

He could have made either of those situations work. But having a civilian here, like this...

*Dammit.*

Maybe she saw someone staring at them. Maybe she had gotten distracted by a ghost. Maybe she was making things up in terror. He didn't know, but the bullshit thing was he had to be sure. Because if she noticed something was off, and she was right, and he didn't pay attention, it would be both their asses on the line.

What the fuck was he going to do?

When he had looked to the right—to his three, for fuck's sake, not his nine—he'd seen the back of a man in a gray suit, but nothing else. He had cut through the crowd, trying to catch up, but there were too many people. People who wanted to shake hands and introduce themselves to him, and find out how he knew the bride and groom. He had a thousand cover stories ready to go, but he couldn't focus on any of them; all he could worry about was how to get through this and make sure the plan was intact. That he was safe to press forward. He should have walked away from this the second he saw the plus one on the invitation.

*Goddammit all to hell.*

The man Piper described fit a description of Rich Chamberlain, that was what was making Damian so edgy. It also fitted the description of a million other rich white guys, and many of them were probably on this damn boat, but if Chamberlain had somehow made him and his cover was blown—well, this job was already going to be hard, but that would have taken it from hard to impossible. At that point, he would grab a lifeboat, take himself and the girl, and row their damn asses back to the shore if necessary. He was a mercenary, and he went where the money was.

He should have burned an ID years ago and gotten away from this. If he was entirely honest with himself, the only reason he didn't was his sister. He couldn't stand the idea of never seeing her again—but more than that, Todd knew her now. If Todd decided to get Damian's attention again, he would do it by hurting Damian's little sister. Damian knew that without question.

"Fucking fuck," Damian muttered under his breath.

He had crossed to the other side of the hall, and the man was gone. He turned around, trying to look like he'd lost sight of a friend, but he knew he was too riled up, too jittery. This was a nightmare in progress, and he didn't know how to get out of it. He had never felt like that before. Like he was on the side of the game where things might not work out the right way. Where he didn't have all the cards up his sleeve and ready to be played.

Because of fucking Todd and his fucking failure to know how to do something right.

That was it. Suddenly, Damian knew what he was going to do. He was going to do his job here, deal with Chamberlain like he'd been hired to do. He would make sure that Piper got her payout—he still had every intention of using her mercilessly, especially if she was going to make him iron hard every time he got a glimpse of her cleavage. And then he would have his guy create an identity for his little sister and her kid, and then he'd make sure they all disappeared.

He hadn't spoken to Alison in years. He had no idea whether or not she would be willing to speak to him. It wasn't like she knew who had paid for the hospital bills. But he had made a career out of being a consummate liar. Something about witness protection, and his connection to her being known, and then he would make it come together.

From what he had seen, she'd never made a solid life for herself in her small town. He doubted she would mind disappearing into the life of the modestly rich and completely not famous—knowing that she would never have to get shoes for the kiddo at a flea market again.

He would do this last job, and then he'd do that. Simple. Plain. Easy.

So why was he standing there, resting his head against the wall and trying to control his breathing, glad that he was out of sight for the moment? Why was his heart pounding?

He knew, and he knew he would never admit it out loud.

# 11

Damian spotted Piper across the way. She drank her wine and ate from her little plate, accepting more hors d'oeuvres whenever a waiter floated by. She wasn't watching Damian as he cut through the crowd; he was her "husband", off to flag down someone for something, which meant she had no reason to worry. No reason to panic. Yet he knew her stomach was probably flipping around like a fish.

She didn't have to stay here, not really. Hell, if Rich Chamberlain was on to Damian, she could go to the man, tell him that Damian was there to fuck with him and ask for some kind of protection in exchange.

But Damian also knew that fear kept her in place because she couldn't be sure. She couldn't be sure, and that meant that she was going to stick with the known quantity. Damian had said he needed her and provided her with compelling proof that he did. She would believe that. At least for now. Until there was a reason to do otherwise.

But her "assignment", for lack of a better word, involved getting close to Fiona. Becoming her friend. That meant that, if necessary, she could reveal herself and Damian, and then ask for protection—say that she'd kept silent for so long out of fear for her life. It certainly wouldn't be a lie.

There was the loud click of a microphone turning on, and the guests all looked around until they spotted the source of the noise. A tall man stood at the front of the hall on a small dais that had been erected. It took Damian a long moment to recognize him. Rich Chamberlain. Whenever his photograph was taken for the society pages or the most recent charity event or the next big Chamber of Commerce award, he had always looked like the kind of guy who could walk out of the office, roll up his sleeves, and keep up in a logging competition. He was strong through the shoulders, narrow through the waist, and just generally a very good-looking guy.

Something had changed now though. He had gotten thin. His suit fit him perfectly, and it added some bulk to his frame without making it look like he was swimming in fabric, but Damian had spent years of his life learning how to see small tricks that changed someone's appearance. Someone had gone to work on his face with makeup as well. It was subtle, beautifully done—as well done as his daughter's really. He looked healthy and strong. But he had lost weight. His cheekbones were sharper, just a bit, and he leaned on the back of a chair as he stood. He made it look casual, but Damian was sure he was using the chair for support.

*What the hell is happening here?*

He didn't think that this was the man Piper had pointed out. His gut said it wasn't. His brain was undecided. Either way, he needed to get back to Piper.

"Thank you so much for joining us," Chamberlain said as Damian threaded his way back through the crowd. "I'm so glad that you could all be here with us as my lovely daughter, Fiona, marries the love of her life, Alex Dodson. I love you, baby."

There was one of those utterly touching and totally staged moments where Chamberlain blew a kiss to his daughter, and she covered her cheeks to hide her smile and brush away the tears in her eyes. Unless they were both really that sappy. That was possible.

Piper had stayed exactly where he'd told her to; point in her favor, then. And she'd done well talking to Fiona. Although something had gone strange there; he'd felt the reaction in the air when Fiona somehow caught Piper off guard. He would have to find out more about that later; now it was time to go back to blending.

Chamberlain kept talking about his daughter, her fiancé, and all the wonderful blessings life had to offer. Damian found the happy husband persona he'd been wearing before and let that slide seamlessly back into place. He was here to do a job. Tearing off like that was foolish; if someone had suspected him, he was surely made now. He'd acted like a damn idiot. His fucking dick was making him overreact. If just being around Piper kept making him react like this, he was going to have to tie her up in their cabin and leave her there.

That thought did not help his dick soften. At all. Gorgeous tanned skin like hers, crisscrossed with rope?

*Damn, that would look absolutely fine.*

When he got back to the table, kissing her like she was the most beautiful woman in the world was easy. She made a soft sound in the back of her throat, and he thought about taking her there and then, making her scream in front of all these hoity-toity people and—what the ever-loving shit was wrong with him?

He broke off the kiss and turned his eyes back to focus on the couple in front of him and the target that he was supposed to eliminate in the next few days. Like the professional that he was.

"I hope you'll all join us in the small ballroom for the wedding," Chamberlain was saying, "while the staff transforms this area into my daughter's daydream. Please." He gestured towards two large doors, which were promptly opened by staff.

People began to move through into a room that was set up to look like a church. *Hell, maybe it is.* Captains were authorized to marry people still, weren't they? Didn't matter—Damian could see the priest from where he was.

The room was set up like a wedding set from a movie. His brain was scrambling to keep up, and all he could do to put himself into the right mindset was to start calculating all the places one would have a clean shot at a target in the front row and to the side, the traditional place that the father of the bride would sit. Even Damian wouldn't shoot a man who was about to kiss his daughter and give her away. Splattering a wedding dress with blood just seemed... wrong. Even if it had made Quentin Tarantino a crap ton of money.

Everyone was directed to seats on the right side of the room, and he and Piper sat down together. The folding chairs were actually comfortable, which was a nice change. You couldn't be as tall as he was without also having a pretty big frame, and he had sat in plenty of chairs that made it seem like he'd gone to the island of Lilliput. This wasn't a chair he was going to relax and spread out in, but it was certainly more comfortable than many he'd used over the years.

The ceremony was brief. He glanced over at Piper a couple of times, but she didn't look like she was on the verge of tears. Her face was pointed towards the couple at the front of the room, but her eyes were unfocused. He knew without question what she was wondering. He leaned over and pressed a light kiss to her neck, just below her ear.

"If you try to get away from me, or you try to tell someone why you think I'm here," he murmured, barely making a noise, "I will find everyone you love. I will hunt them down and exterminate them. Don't think of crossing me. Are we clear?"

She flinched a little, and the glance she turned towards him was one of muted terror. But she turned back to the couple, and this time, she focused all of her attention where it needed to be.

*Good girl.*

That thought surprised him, just a little. But he also had to own that she was holding up well. The average girl who had been basically kidnapped, pushed into sex that she didn't want just to ease someone else's nerves, and then told to pretend to be someone she wasn't—most girls couldn't handle that. Not bad, especially for a girl who, to the best of his knowledge, was just a regular girl.

He watched the wedding ceremony, but it didn't really make much of an impact. Too many of his clients were husbands and wives who'd had enough and wanted a quick out that would satisfy their prenup. He'd gotten very good at a million different things—faking someone else's cheating, cons that ended in both parties satisfied, and, in extreme cases, poisons that were virtually impossible to detect. It was hard to look at something like this and think romance. Maybe poor people got married without planning on scamming each other out of everything. Once you started working with rich people, though, all bets were off.

He looked for the man that Piper might have seen and surveyed the crowd. There were fewer people than he had expected on the boat, and he was more relieved than ever that he'd made sure his "plus one" had shown up as expected. Everyone here was coupled; he would have stood out like a sore thumb as a single man.

Fiona had one bridesmaid, who looked to be much older than she was. Alex had a best man, about his age. There was something awkward about the best man; he shifted his feet and studied the guests in a way that felt almost nervous. Well, maybe he didn't like being in front of crowds. He certainly would not be the first person who thought it would be fine, then broke into a sweat up there, even if they weren't really the person being watched.

Still, it pinged on Damian's radar. It might be as minor as "the best man was secretly in love with the bride", but it might be something more.

There were the "I do" vows, and then the kiss, and cheers, and the bride and groom went back down the aisle while everyone applauded and reached out to touch them as if the love would rub off on them. As if love were something tangible, or even real.

Before the guests could start to leave, Chamberlain was up at the front of the room again, his arms spread, talking about how beautiful his daughter was. It was painfully obvious that he was covering for the newly married couple, giving them a quick minute to catch their breath—and maybe have the quickest of quickies—before the transformed ballroom turned into a reception where they would be "performing happiness" for hours.

Damian only half listened to what Chamberlain was saying; it was clear the man loved his daughter more than anything, and that he was sentimental about everything that was happening, but that was all that Damian was catching. It was good information that Fiona would be useful leverage if needed, but there wasn't more than that to hear.

He glanced over at Piper, who finally had tears shining in her eyes. What about this father's speech was more moving than the wedding itself? Of course, she was recently broken up; it was very possible that she was just as bitter about the concept of loving "til death do you part" as he was. Why set yourself up for unrealistic goals? It just seemed stupid.

He reached down and squeezed her hand, giving her a small, warm smile. That was what the loving husband would do, right? But she leaned into him, placed her head on his shoulder and her free hand on his arm. Something in him was suddenly confused. Was she pretending? Or was there something else going on?

And why the hell did he want to wrap his arm around her shoulders and kiss the top of her head?

He took a deep breath and hardened the part of himself that was trying so hard to go soft for no goddamn reason.

When they eventually moved back into the transformed ballroom, Damian was impressed. The room had been stately and formal before; now it looked like the site of a high school prom but dialed up with class—draped fabric, chairs with bows, plates with half a dozen pieces of silverware, and, instead of a head table, a small sweetheart table that stood under an archway decorated with roses. Whoever was the wedding planner was doing an amazing job keeping up with the rapid-fire demands of this event. Event planners and con men were the only people he had ever seen transform spaces this rapidly. He could absolutely believe that they'd just entered a completely different space—if he didn't have the knack of looking around and seeing the shape of a room beyond its decorations.

He held Piper's hand as they looked for their assigned seats.

## 12

Piper had always found weddings to be, in general, bullshit. Her parents had divorced when she was little, and while she had hoped that would stop the screaming and fighting it, well, it simply hadn't. She had never figured that relationships really needed rubber stamps from the government to be official, though she'd figured that, eventually, she would sign the papers for the tax benefits—if she found the right person. And she was pretty sure she wanted kids eventually; that part was definitely easier if you had the pieces of legal paper all organized.

But the whole doe-eyed in a white dress thing? That part hadn't ever done much for her.

Hearing Fiona's dad up there, however, talking about how beautiful his daughter was and how proud of her he was? That part had turned her inside out. It wasn't that her own father hadn't been there for her, and damn did she ever hate the term "daddy issues", but she'd never been close to her father.

Reaching out to Damian for reassurance had been strange, but it had also been right. As gross and wrong as it felt, he was the only person she had right now. And, as they said, "Any port in a storm."

There was something dark in him, and the more she looked at him, the darker it seemed to get. She had started out thinking he was here for some kind of con that would compromise Chamberlain. She didn't know why a person would want to do that; as far as she knew, Chamberlain was a pillar of the community, solid businessman, all of that—but people were people, and everyone wanted something. Someone would gain something, most likely if he were—what? Dethroned? Tarnished? Lost his fortune?

*Died?*

That last one scared her somehow. She didn't know the man and wasn't personally involved if he died, but the idea that the man next to her might be the one with a plan to kill him... that terrified her.

The shock and fear of everything that had happened since stepping outside of Marissa's apartment were finally catching up to Piper. She wished she had her purse, and the small bottle of anti-anxiety pills her doctor had prescribed for her occasional panic.

Everything was hazy, and she clung to Damian's hand as he took them to a table. She ate food when it was in front of her and was distantly aware that it was good. She clapped when everyone else clapped and made sure she was always looking in the direction of whoever was talking. But she wasn't taking in very much at all. She was overwhelmed, and she desperately needed to go someplace quiet for a little while until the storm of emotions inside of her calmed down.

There was dancing. Damian asked her if she wanted to dance, and she shook her head. He kissed her softly, looking for all the world like a caring husband. She wasn't wearing a ring. What was her story if someone noticed the ring? He hadn't planned for that, and she should mention it later. See what he thought.

She blinked, and then Fiona was standing in front of her, holding out her hands. Piper stood, taking the other woman's hands and smiling into her brilliantly happy face. And then she saw something so sharp and shocking that she was surprised she hadn't seen it before.

Fiona was heartbroken. She was on the verge of tears and had been for a while now. Her eyes were reddened, and she looked worn thin. Maybe she'd just had a long day, but there was something more. Piper doubted she would have been able to see it if she wasn't stretched so thin herself; she certainly hadn't noticed it earlier.

"It's so good to see you," Fiona was saying. "I can't believe we lost touch after school."

Piper smiled and nodded, but she couldn't figure it out. She knew damn well that she had never met Fiona before today; why in the world was the girl pretending that she and Piper had been friends?

"I'd like to catch up tomorrow, if that's alright?"

"Of-of course," Piper said. "Do you want me to meet you somewhere?"

"Sure." Fiona's voice was way too chipper. Her eyes were bright, and the way she was forcing her emotions was so painfully clear. "There's a small cafe on the forward deck. Do you think you could meet me there in the morning? Maybe around nine?"

That was absurdly early for a new bride who was going to spend all night with her new husband, wasn't it? It seemed truly ridiculous.

"My pleasure," Piper said.

"I have to go." Fiona shot a look over her shoulder at her waiting husband and gave a smile that didn't come anywhere near her eyes. "I'll see you then."

She didn't wait for Piper's goodbye before she walked away.

Piper watched her go and was more confused than ever. She sat down in her chair and glanced at Damian, who had leaned in to give her a kiss on the cheek. He whispered in her ear; this was becoming a pattern:

"I want to get back to our room as soon as possible," he said, his voice low. "I think there's an assassin on this boat."

Another pause.

"I mean, besides me."

Piper tried to keep her shock under control as they walked quickly back to their cabin. Every so often, Damian stopped and pushed her against something, groping her and kissing her hard, as if they were just desperate to get somewhere with a flat surface and fuck.

At one point, he caught her bare thigh, lifting it up around his waist, and she thought he really might fuck her right there. She knew she couldn't have stopped him. She wasn't sure that she would have tried. Her body wanted him, but her head just wasn't paying attention to anything other than the words he said.

*An assassin other than him.*

So much for the long con, the guy trying to make a good stock deal, or some other shady but not illegal business. Damian was here for a very specific, and very bloody purpose.

Two things were turning her stomach: first, she wasn't surprised at all. Something about his cold eyes and the way he watched her so closely had left her sure that something was going on since they had first met.

But the second frightened her more: she didn't seem to care. She wanted him just as much as she had before. She knew that if he tried to fuck her again, she would try to fight him off. She needed to believe that she wasn't the sort of girl who could crave a murderer.

But here she was, and there wasn't really any way around what was happening. She was soaking wet, thinking of how he had used her as "stress relief" before, and even though she'd hated it, she wanted more.

So when he pushed her up against the wall and lifted her leg, she slid her hand between them, cupping his cock and stroking him through his pants. He hissed into her mouth and moved harder against her.

"Don't worry, Piper," he said. "We'll get to that. I need it just as much as you do. Don't worry."

He rammed three fingers into her without warning, thrust half a dozen times while she tried not to scream, and then pulled them free, leaving her aching and empty and wanting him so much more.

He let her go and walked down the hallway, leaving her to follow. She did. There was one moment where she felt disgraced, like a puppy left behind to trail behind its master, but then maybe 'master' was a good word for him. She didn't hesitate for a second before she trotted along.

In the bedroom, that thin veneer of social acceptability that he had been wearing dropped like a stone. His face went flat, his eyes cold, and his movements became brisk and efficient. He didn't seem to even realize Piper was still in the room. She watched him standing at the cabin door, then went to sit down. She was still wet and aching, and she pressed her thighs together to get a little pressure.

He went immediately to the suitcases that had been brought on board with them. He opened them and checked over certain areas of the clothing. She didn't know what he was looking for, but when he found—or didn't find—it, he breathed a sigh of relief.

"I need to unpack things and check my gear," he said, his voice still flat. "And you are going to keep me entertained while I do it."

"I—What?"

"You heard me. I already took your panties. Hook your feet on that coffee table, so you're spread nice and wide. And play with yourself. You can come, but you'll have to keep fucking yourself afterward, no matter how much it hurts. Do you understand? If you try and stop, believe me, I'll make it hurt a thousand times worse."

Piper swallowed. "I... I'm sorry, but I don't understand?"

He turned towards her. His eyes didn't warm, but he waited for her to ask whatever question she had.

"I don't—My fingers aren't enough. I'm not going to get off like that."

He shrugged. "Then torture yourself. If you're lucky, I'll help when I'm done with what I'm doing. Or maybe knowing that you're being watched by someone who doesn't care how you feel will help. It doesn't matter to me. But if you stop—" He slowed down and made a deeply satisfied sound. "If you stop, I'll use my belt on your swollen cunt. And you have no idea how much I will enjoy that. I'll whip you until I feel better. No matter what you say. And believe me, I love listening to a girl try not to scream." Another pause and his face broke into a vicious grin. "Maybe I'll stuff your soaked panties into your mouth and listen to you try to beg around them, hmm?"

Piper didn't say another word. She shifted back on the couch, into a more comfortable position, then hooked her feet, just like he had said. She pulled the skirt of her dress up high; it was still under her ass, but her cunt was completely exposed. Her cheeks flushed thinking of how she must look, how wanton. How slutty. Was her cunt really swollen like he said?

She didn't have a problem with using her fingers to play with herself; they would just never been enough. But the thought of his belt made her cringe. She didn't have to come; she just had to be entertaining.

She reached between her legs and slid her fingers up her slit. She was soaking wet, and yes, she was swollen and thick, from her clit to the bottom of her lips. It was different than she had ever felt. Instead of the dry, just barely full feeling, her hips arched with the brush of her fingers, and she responded with a gasp. He looked up, his gaze cold, but lingering.

She ran her fingers from bottom to top again as he took each item of clothing out of the suitcases and placed them to the side. There was a level of care there she appreciated. She ran her fingers around her clit and sighed at the gentle sensations that ran through her. Another circle made her arch into her fingers.

His gaze towards her again made her body heat up. She wanted more, and she teased her fingers around her opening as he continued to go through his suitcase methodically. When he started to pull out pieces of metal that she recognized as guns, her fingers faltered.

"Don't stop," he said without looking at her. "I wasn't joking about the belt. Unless that's what you want?"

He kept unloading things, guns and sights and other things she didn't know the name of. It was... strange—continuing to touch herself while he held such violent tools in his hands. She wished she could stop, and she found herself wondering how much it could possibly hurt to have the leather crack down on her cunt. The thought of it made her whimper quietly.

She was teasing a finger inside her aching cunt when Damian nodded in quiet satisfaction. Some sort of stress eased out of his shoulders, and he took a long, slow breath.

"Everything's where it should be here," he said. "Good." He turned and looked at her, and his gaze was just as cold as it had been. "Stop."

Her fingers froze, then slipped back to one thigh. She was left wanting, but in a different way than before. She felt calm, cool. She wanted to come but more softly. With less desperation.

"Come over here," he said, snapping his fingers and pointing at the bed in front of him.

She stood, hesitant for just a moment, then moved more quickly. She sat where he pointed, her knees together and her hands neatly in her lap.

"We need to talk."

Piper nodded. "You said there was another assassin on the boat. That means you're here to kill someone."

Damian sighed. "You thought it was something else?"

"I thought... Like on that *Leverage* TV show or something."

That actually made the hard-ass crack a smile. She thought it was real, this time. He had a decent smile. One that made him look... something that could pass as kind.

"I wish it were," he said. "But no. I've done that kind of work, sure, but when I'm hired, usually it's to make someone disappear. Permanently."

"And this time it's Rich Chamberlain?"

Damian nodded.

"Why? He seems like a good man. Does he have some dirty past or some—some hooker with a baby? What the hell is going on?" Piper's voice was tight, high.

She didn't recognize it herself. The need in her clit intensified, as if the conversation, the potential for viciousness was making her hotter.

"The Santiagos want him dead," Damian said, the same way that he had mentioned that he had a great cookie recipe from his grandma. "I don't think past that. They pay me well enough that it's not necessary."

But there was something in his voice that said this was a lie. She couldn't quite pinpoint the part that didn't feel true, but everything else he'd said to her, even when he was being someone else, had felt calm and confident. This was different.

"Why am I here? Is it really just about Fiona?"

"The Santiagos put me on this boat without a plan. We have a little bit of time before we turn back around to shore. We'll be in international waters for three days, which makes committing a crime a very different proposition. I've got a good reputation. I come up with plans, and that's not a problem. But this time—this time I don't have much of a plan. And I don't have a lot of time. I don't need complications."

"And I'm a complication?"

He shrugged. "I'm over that. You did good back there—spotting the guy watching us. You're going to be an asset."

"So the complication?"

"That guy. He left too smooth. And he was watching us in certain ways... It could be that I'm being too paranoid, but I don't think he was on the up and up. And maybe someone else is here for Chamberlain."

"That's a lot of people trying to kill one decent guy."

Damian shrugged again, and there was something about it that made Piper's guts twist up.

"Just because you and I don't know what's wrong with him, that doesn't mean there's nothing wrong with him. You have to remember that in this business. Lots of people look fine, but no one's solid good, all the way down."

Piper weighed the benefits of trying to get more information against her real fear that if she pissed Damian off enough, that coldness in him might come to the forefront again, and that this time it might find its release in hurting her. Not like before; the kind he had threatened with his belt; the kind that could kill her if he decided to stray from the kind of sexual play he'd mentioned.

There were guns on the bed. She had seen him check them, and she was pretty sure that meant they were unloaded, but this was not a time to antagonize him.

"Is it okay—me asking all these questions?" She made her voice small and a little timid, trying to seem helpless.

If he didn't think she was any kind of threat, would that make her safer? Or would he think she was stupid and just dispose of her outright? It wasn't hard to make her voice shake; her fear was becoming more and more real with every breath.

He made a vague gesture with his hand. He had gone back to the weaponry laid out in front of him. There weren't just guns; she saw knives and the length of wire with hand grips that people got choked with in James Bond films. She also saw other things that she hadn't expected: a tiny box of electronics that looked like it might be some kind of—it was either a bomb or a computer, it was hard for her to be entirely sure; a leather roll that, if movies were ever true at all, would hold lockpicks; and other stuff she couldn't even guess at.

"At least that fucker got my whole kit here." Damian glanced at her, and a little more of that coldness had faded.

He reached out and pushed her legs apart, sitting down next to her. He didn't trace his fingers up her thighs or bother with any kind of romance. He didn't play with her to see if she was wet; he pushed three fingers inside of her cunt and made her whimper with the sudden pain of it.

"Go ahead," he said, shifting his fingers inside of her, spreading them, adding to the pain of the invasion with a harsh stretching. "Ask your questions."

It hurt, and she was scared. She wanted to pull away, crawl up the bed and beg him to stop. Grab his arm and try to shove him away. But her hips weren't listening to any of that. They were shifting with his tiny thrusts, eager and begging for more of his rough treatment. Being scared and being desperate for him to fuck her hard and sore mixed, leaving her with a potent emotional stew that burned her up inside.

He gave her a light slap with his free hand.

"You have questions. Ask them." His voice was kind, soft. Conversational. His hands were the only brutal things.

"The Santiagos—" As soon as she started to speak, his hand moved faster, twisting more.

She felt him push another finger inside of her and she tried not to scream. It hurt so much, she was too full, and her hips were bucking wildly. On the couch, she had felt a strange warmth against her own touch that had surprised her. She'd never played with herself much, just occasionally used a cheap vibrator to rub out a quick orgasm when she was watching a movie that made her wet, or when she read a book that made her squirm and push her thighs together. This was something entirely different, bigger, more, and she wanted all of it.

"You stop, and I stop," he said with that same conversational tone. "And then I whip your ass black and blue. You're going to come on my fingers because it hurts, or I'm going to come on your bright red ass. You fucking pick."

"The Santiagos," she started again.

She forced her attention on forming her words, and not the swirling need that was moving down to her clit. She was going to come like this if he kept this up, and she tried to feel shame about that. Instead, she just felt want. If talking were what kept him moving, then she would talk.

"I know they're—crime in the city. They are behind—fuck—things like the drugs and the—I don't really know what else. But wh —"

He slammed his fingers into her hard, this thumb strumming her clit, and her whole body convulsed as she let out a little cry. She had to force herself to keep speaking, no matter how much she just wanted to ride the pleasure and scream until it crested.

"Why do they give a shit about this one man?"

Damian didn't answer; just finger-fucked her harder while she writhed, trying to get more leverage. The angle was awkward, and after a minute, he shoved her down, spreading her out on the bed. He knelt on her thighs, one arm bracing himself while the other slammed into her harder and harder. She was meeting every thrust with a little scream now, forcing herself to wait as long as she could. The pleasure built and built and built like water behind a dam, and then he snarled.

"Come for me, you pretty bitch."

She couldn't wait another second. She felt her body lock down around his fingers, her hips arching up against his weight. She couldn't scream, she knew she couldn't, but she couldn't be quiet. She clenched her teeth and let only the most strangled sounds out of her mouth.

He kept fucking her through the crest, and kept fucking her and flicking her clit even as the orgasm passed and the spasms of pleasure rolled through her and started to settle. He kept doing it, even when she cursed and whimpered and tried to get away from how much it hurt.

Damian eventually pulled his fingers free from her with the most whore-ish wet sound, then ran his fingers over her lips.

"Taste yourself," he said, and she opened her mouth without considering whether it was what she wanted.

She sucked them as thoroughly as she would have sucked his cock if he had shoved it in her face at that moment. She tasted salty and warm, and underneath the musk of her cunt, she tasted something different. The flavor of his skin.

*God...* She liked that.

"To answer your question," he said, sitting back as if he hadn't just finger-fucked her until she was desperately forcing back screams, "it's hard to say. Like I said, I don't get a lot of information when I get a job, just what I need to complete the assignment. Of course, I did independent research, but I wasn't given anything like the lead time I needed to make this happen as clean as I want."

She was floating on a cloud of lust and relaxation; if she wasn't stretched out next to a man who was completely comfortable with his profession as a contract killer, she might have considered a brief nap. That wasn't an option though. She pushed herself up to a sitting point and folded her skirt back down over her knees. He raised an eyebrow at her primness; he was definitely laughing at her.

"So what do you know?"

He sighed, scrubbing his hand through his hair. "I can't find details. But I wouldn't be surprised if one of Chamberlain's business interests is backing something political that will mess with the Santiagos' business. There have been more of those lately. The crime world has changed—it's not all loan sharking and intimidation and buying politicians now. There are cyber currency and long cons and payday loans and, well, it's all the same crimes, but they're dressed up in different ways. The Santiagos aren't evolving, and they're getting left behind. I know Chamberlain supports the kind of politicians who are more difficult to buy. The kind who mean it when they say they want to clean up the city."

"Supports them and donates to them?"

"Yeah, seems like that."

She shrugged. "I'm no criminal mastermind, but it seems like that's enough of a reason to off someone when you're a, you know, known gangster."

Damian nodded. "It's just such a bad move. Killing politicians because they're against you is so... 1920s. Nowadays, you engineer a scandal, you use dark money against them, you... do one of a million other things."

Piper raised an eyebrow. "Must be hard for an honest mercenary to make a living."

"A man uses what talents he has to make what living he can."

"And you have a talent for killing."

Damian sighed and flopped onto his back.

After a moment, Piper gathered herself and rolled onto her side, watching him.

"No," he said. "At least, it's not as simple as that. I'm ex-military. Not, I imagine, a surprise. When I got out, I went into private security—that's where the money is for guys like me. And I took some side jobs because everyone takes side jobs. But then my sister got sick, and I needed a lot of money, fast. I called in some markers to get a couple of contacts, did a few jobs, but there wasn't enough insurance, and never enough money. I'd done work for the Santiagos before, but once Todd got his hooks into me..." He sighed.

Piper shivered. Todd had always seemed so plain and boring to her. At first, that had been part of his appeal. Someone strong, stable, and reliable. She would come home every night, and he would be there. Thinking about the life he could have pulled her into... Of course, he already had done that, hadn't he?

*Bastard.*

"What about you?" Damian asked, looking at her differently.

It was funny. Even though she was a complete, fucked, silly mess, he was looking at her like an... actual person.

"Before you got pulled into all of this, what were you doing?" he added.

Piper shrugged. "I'm kind of a consultant. I work with businesses—helping them get set up with crowdfunding stuff, trying to help them be more successful, give them a better chance to succeed. Todd thought it was boring, and that I should do something that would earn more money?"

"Did it do good? What you were doing?"

Piper thought over her clients. So many of them were women who were trying to get together capital to start or expand businesses, or crowdfund art projects, or do other things that the rest of the world wanted to keep them from doing. It sounded silly to the rest of the world, but it had never felt silly to her.

"I think it did," she said. "I think it helped some people get the start they wouldn't have had otherwise."

"Then Todd was even more of an asshole than I thought." Something in Damian's eyes darkened, and he reached for her hand, pulling it over to rest on his cock. He hadn't ever bothered to zip up again after before, and she shivered at the way he felt—velvet over steel, hard as a rock. "Tell me something, baby. Did he have a hard cock like this?"

Piper shook her head. She traced her hand lightly over him, and he pressed her hand down firmer, arcing up into her touch with a little hiss.

"Say it," he said.

"What?" Piper knew what he wanted to hear, but she wanted to tease, just a little. "That he had a useless little pecker?"

"Yeah. Did he ever fuck you right?"

"Not once." Piper stroked her hand harder, and he shifted his hips under her hand.

He shoved his pants down and out of the way, then pulled his shirt up over his head. He reached for her. She went to unzip her dress, and he slapped her hands away. He pulled her over him, took a moment to position himself at her entrance, and then pushed up into her so hard that she let out another little cry.

It didn't matter how wet she was; it hurt every time he thrust into her. After the last time, she was tight and sore, and it hurt to have him inside of her again, but she could see by the look on his face that he didn't care. And she couldn't have convinced herself to ask him to stop anyway.

"Is this how you like to be fucked?" He shoved himself up into her more, and she moved her hips to take him as deep as she could, even though it made her cry out.

"Yes," she said, biting back a scream.

"Good."

He slammed her down again and again until she felt his balls tighten, and then the convulsions of his cock as he came inside of her. She almost wished she would come with him, yet her cunt was so sore and aching that she wasn't sure it would have been possible.

He moved her off of him with more gentleness than she might have expected. He traced her cheek with one finger, smiling just a little. "Clean up if you want, then get some sleep. I've got work to do, and I'll be gone most of the night. If you're spending time with Fiona tomorrow, I need you bright eyed and bushy tailed."

Piper nodded, feeling almost numb. She pushed herself up and went to the suitcases. She had to give Todd one thing; he knew what sizes she wore, and he'd gone out of his way to provide her with some beautiful clothes for this trip. She found a T-shirt and some comfortable looking pajama bottoms, then headed for the bathroom.

It had been one hell of a long day, and she needed to feel clean and then get some damn rest.

## 13

Damian watched Piper leave the room and felt the softness melt away from him. That was good. He shouldn't be allowing himself even this much luxury. Just because she made his dick feel good wasn't a reason to fall for her. He had to be better than this. He would get both of them killed if he weren't.

He wet a cloth in the suite's small kitchen to clean himself up. He reeked of sex, and it made him feel weak. Distracted. As the smell faded, his sense of purpose focused. He'd blown it off when Piper had commented that he had a talent for killing, but the truth was that he did. He didn't know if it made him some sort of sociopath or psychopath, but he'd gotten farther in the military because it didn't hurt him to rack up kills the way it did some men. He was sure those men were better people than he was, and weirdly, he was glad of it. Someone had to be the one to neutralize targets, and better him than some guy who would be going home to a wife and kids wracked with PTSD and unable to get help.

Private security hadn't fed the monster inside him, the vicious beast that hungered for blood and violence. People always thought of private security as protecting the target from monsters that appeared from a dozen directions. He'd had a few days like that, of course, but most of the time, his days had droned on, standing in front of places with dark glasses and ill-fitting earpieces, exhausting himself by being endlessly on edge. He had started taking jobs on the side, and they were more lucrative than anything he'd done in the legitimate side of business. And his sister needed help.

Someone in his family had to stay alive, and human.

He dressed in dark clothes that would make him blend into shadows without looking like some kind of monster if he had to talk to someone like a guest. No tactical vest or utility belt. Still, he was good at hiding weapons in his shirt sleeves, tucking lockpicks in his belt, and generally keeping whatever he needed on his person whenever he needed to do so.

The water in the shower came on, and he left the room, locking the door behind him. He gave himself one minute to worry about Piper, concerned that she might be in danger without him there to protect her, but he needed to do his job. Long term, that was going to be the best thing for her. Do his job, do it right, and then get them both off this boat and back to the rest of the world. She could go back to her life, and he would do the same.

The boat was mostly quiet now. He heard the music playing in the reception, so there were only a few people left in that space to make noise. Most people would have gone back to their cabins, either to fuck or sleep. It had been a long day for most people, he imagined, and with an open bar, people had more than indulged.

He went over his mental list. He needed to locate Chamberlain's cabin, set up surveillance, and see who else had space nearby. Determine who, if anyone, was sharing the cabin. Find out the information he needed to make a plan. All the shit he should have known long before he set foot onboard.

Damian sighed and kept still until the irritation washed off him again. He'd never had so much trouble maintaining that inner stillness, not since his earliest days in the military. He had trained himself to do better than this. Hell if he was going to let one girl screw it all up inside his head, even if she was an incredibly good lay. He would use her the same way he'd use his hand—something to keep him from being distracted by an inconvenient boner—and let her be nothing else.

Except that wasn't going to be really possible, now was it? He needed her, and that meant he had to pay attention to her and make sure she was capable.

*Dammit all to hell.*

Damn Todd and his stupid vengeance games instead of doing what needed to be done and getting Damian the professional assistance he required. If Damian went down for this somehow, he would find a way to take Todd down with him. There was no other option.

Damian made his way through the decks of the ship, mapping out everything from the crew quarters to the upper decks. There were several places he figured a wealthy old man might frequent. There was a top-shelf bar, for example, designed more like a gentleman's club than the usual plain drinking affair. There was a regular bar as well a deck down. It didn't have as much of a view, but it was much friendlier to simply get drunk.

There was a small store for clothing with a range of items from the sort of thing a man would wear to a fine dinner to basic toiletries. It was unlikely that Chamberlain would spend much time there—unless he ran out of toothpaste or something. And even then, surely, he had people for that.

Damian also found the places where Chamberlain would have the best views of different areas. And that was where things started to get strange. There was a crow's nest of sorts that gave a great view of the deck below, from the pool area to the dining section towards the back of the ship. It was unkempt compared to the more common areas of the boat. He had expected to pick the lock at the top of the stairs, but the door was already open. It was possible a crew member had come up here, but it seemed unlikely, and if they'd stolen a key, they would have locked the door behind them. Similarly, if he had picked the lock, he would have used his picks to lock it behind him again—if necessary.

There was a fine layer of dust on the small deck, and signs that someone had come up here, crouched and looked around. They had smoked a few cigarettes—not all of them tobacco—and hadn't gotten rid of the butts. They'd chosen a spot that an amateur would think was a great lookout, but it was obvious to Damian that the person was visible from the pool area, if not the dining area. Moving one corner over would give much better cover.

Even more importantly, a sniper rifle would eject its rounds out of the crow's nest from that point, meaning that the person wouldn't be able to collect the evidence on their way out of the area. He could see the telltale marks of a tripod set up, and he felt sure that someone had been up here with a scope, looking around and trying to find the right way to shoot someone down in the dining area.

*Sloppy. Just fucking sloppy.*

If there was another shooter on this boat and Todd knew about it; Damian was going to shoot the son of a bitch where he stood.

Damian hesitated for a long moment, then pulled a burner phone out of his pocket. He put in the SIM card, then powered the phone on. Remarkably, he had reception. He tapped out a quick message to Todd—and after a moment, added Carlos to the message:

*Potential company on board. Friend of yours? Should I introduce myself?*

As soon as he saw that the message had sent, he powered the phone off. He would check for a response later. Now, he needed to see the cabin area.

He went back down the stairs after relocking the door at the top. He considered leaving it unlocked, just in case it really had been a crew member who had done it, and his nemesis was just lucky. But, in the end, that seemed so unlikely that locking it behind him was the obvious right choice.

Damian made his way back down the decks, heading towards the forward cabins with the best views and most luxurious spaces. No one bothered him or tried to stop him. He didn't even have to creep and hide in the shadows. That was what people didn't realize—as long as you acted like you belonged where you were, few people would bother to try and stop you. They would barely notice you and would forget you quickly. It made his job a thousand times easier. He always appreciated the little shortcuts.

As he got closer to the suites, there were private security guys. They weren't subtle; they stood in corners and beside doors, hands crossed loosely in front of them, dark glasses hiding where they were looking and earpieces obvious. He'd had a few jobs where they weren't even active, but having them there somehow intimidated people. Damian had never quite understood why.

For a moment, he felt sorry for the men. He wondered if they were happy in the job, guarding a rich bastard from whatever he might be facing, or if they were as bored as he had been standing in doorways just like this one.

They had certainly clocked him; he saw the slight tightening of their shoulders, the minor shifting of their hands towards whatever weapons they were carrying. He couldn't convincingly play off being drunk at this point, so he went for the simplest exit he could. He let himself skid to a halt like he had been surprised by what he saw.

"Hey, sorry, boys," he said, laughing just a little. He turned his face into that of a regular guy, grinning and laughing. Maybe he'd been drinking, wandering the ship to get his sea legs, and had taken a wrong turn. "Was walking and got a little lost. Sorry."

He played at being as uncomfortable as someone would be when they suddenly saw a handful of men who were clearly carrying weapons. He awkwardly turned, letting his feet stumble, and looked back a couple times as if he was afraid they would follow him. They maintained their tension, but it was perfunctory; he had been assessed and determined not to be a threat.

*Amateurs. This entire boat is full of goddamned amateurs.*

He turned down a couple of hallways, exploring and mapping, but stopped short when he heard two men arguing. Before he could even hear the words, he knew they weren't two drunk men arguing about who was fucking which bridesmaid.

After a moment, he recognized one of the voices; Alex, the recent groom. Damian was surprised, and a little disappointed in the man. Fiona had looked a little vanilla for his tastes, but she was certainly worth more than just the few hours since the wedding. Of course, maybe she was tired and had gone to sleep. These days, it wasn't like the wedding night was the first time for many couples anyway.

Without thinking, Damian slipped into the shadows, all the facades he wore throughout the day fading away. He made himself into darkness, just disappearing, and moved closer to the two men. The carpeted floor made his footfalls quieter anyway, but he wouldn't have made a sound on a floor made of marbles. He had trained for moments like this one.

Just around the corner from where they were arguing was a small alcove with a tastefully appointed vending machine, an ice machine, and packets of coffee grounds in a dozen flavors and roasts. He would have preferred something darker, but he tucked himself between the wall and the vending machine and felt fairly sure that he was invisible—unless someone really wanted a Snickers. He listened carefully to the words coming at him from the hallway.

"Chris, what are you thinking?" Alex snapped, his voice tense and low. "She'll wake up and notice I'm gone, and how do you think that fucking conversation is going to go?"

"I don't give a shit," the other man—Chris—said. "You told me that there wouldn't be security. That this would be an easy job. I would have doubled my fee if I'd known it would be like this."

"Whatever. The old man changed his plans. I can't be held responsible for that. You do your job, or you won't get off this boat."

An empty threat; Damian heard it at once. The tremor in the other man's voice, and the slight shake—he hadn't ever killed someone. He probably wasn't even carrying a weapon, and he wouldn't know how to land a killing blow quickly if he did.

*Nonsense.*

This Chris bastard didn't have Damian's instincts.

"Okay, man, calm down, alright? I just—I don't have the right equipment to get around this stuff."

Alex's voice was more heated. "What do you think I'm paying you for. Figure it the hell out. Now I'm getting back to my wife."

There was the rough sound of one man shoving past another, and a body hitting a wall. Not with a lot of force, just the movement of someone being pushed aside.

Damian stayed still as Alex stomped down the hallway away from him. After another set of low curses, Damian heard Chris moving in the opposite direction.

*Well. That certainly made things more interesting.*

Damian made the quick choice to follow Chris at a distance and find out which cabin he was in; the guy didn't even glance up as Damian traced his steps. He slammed his cabin door behind him, loud enough to irritate someone awake, but only if they were paying attention and listening for odd sounds. The doors were well cushioned and closed slowly and gently.

*Convenient, good to know...*

But also, it would make it harder to make a quick and subtle exit from a room if needed. Damian counted down the three seconds it took for the door to close and made a mental note to check his own door and see if the time was consistent.

Damian crept through the ship more, finding nooks and small spots to hide gear if necessary and unexpected passages that led from one place to another. They were clearly designed to let staff move quickly throughout the ship, but they were dusty and disused. Perfect for him.

When he got back to his cabin, he unlocked the door, slipped in quickly—the door closing time was consistent—and stripped down to his boxers as he headed towards the bed. It wasn't until he saw the body stretched out under the covers that he remembered he was sharing the room with someone.

He cursed quietly—enough that he wouldn't wake Piper up—and then tried to decide what to do. He certainly hadn't told her that she shouldn't sleep in the bed, and he wasn't enough of a bastard to wake her up and kick her to the couch. But at the same time, he was tired and wanted a good night's sleep. Tomorrow could go a lot of different ways, and he would be better off fresh.

It only took a few moments to make the call. Piper looked to be a neat sleeper. She was curled to one side of the bed, and she wasn't snoring. He grabbed an extra blanket from the closet and laid down on top of the covers, pulling the blanket over himself. He felt like a real gentleman, which was bizarre as hell. He wasn't sure he had ever felt like that before.

But it didn't take him long to fall asleep. It never did.

## 14

Piper woke slowly, awareness gradually fading back in. She remembered where she was, bit by bit, and was lulled by the gentle motion of the ship on the water. And then the remembering of why she was on the ship in the first place rushed back into her all at once, and she jerked upright with her hand pressed against her sternum as if she could use it to calm her racing heart.

She squeezed her eyes shut and tried to focus on her breathing, on pulling her energy back down to a level where her heart wouldn't feel as if it were trying to break through her ribs.

When she could take a deep breath, she opened her eyes again. Just to the side of her, Damian was wide awake but still. It looked like he had laid down on top of the comforter, but with a blanket pulled over him. It was the strangest thing she'd ever seen, but it made her feel weirdly safer.

"Sorry," she said. "I don't normally... do that when I wake up."

He nodded slowly. "I normally wake up exactly like this. Well, sometimes there's a gun." Piper felt the blood drain from her cheeks, and Damian laughed. "Kidding. Promise. I'm kidding."

He sat up and stretched, and Piper enjoyed seeing the flat planes of his chest. She wanted to run her hands over them, maybe following them with her tongue. He was terrifying, and he was the hottest man she had ever seen.

"Did you learn anything last night, while you were... out?"

He nodded, scrubbing his hands through his hair. "There's someone else here. Staking the place out. Looking for opportunities. But they're sloppy as hell."

"That's good, isn't it?"

"Not even remotely."

She stared at his tight ass. She had spent time with her hands on it yesterday, but she hadn't gotten to *see* it. Apparently, every inch of him was as perfectly carved as his chest and abs. No part of this was supposed to make her as wet as it was.

"If the dumb jackass runs around and gets caught, everyone gets on edge. Chamberlain already has private security on board—having extra attention on the ship puts extra attention on me. That's the last thing I need." He shook his head. "This is going to be a mess as it is."

Piper nodded. She'd had a long time to think last night—showering and then getting into bed when Damian was gone. She had realized that, no matter what else happened, he was probably the only way she was getting off this boat. If she tried to betray him, she had no doubt that he would kill her and toss her overboard without a second thought. She needed to do what he said, get through this, and then she'd run for it. Hell, if the police caught him, she would say that he'd kidnapped her. It certainly wouldn't be a lie. She'd throw Todd under the bus as well, just as hard.

But, in the meantime, if she could be helpful, if she could make sure he got done what he needed to get done without getting caught... her life would be that much easier. She didn't like the idea of what he was here for, but if her choice was to live or die herself... She chose to live. Maybe that made her a coward. She didn't care.

"When I'm with Fiona today..." Piper started.

Damian turned back to her, and she saw his cock outlined against his tight shorts. She forced herself not to lick her lips. It wasn't easy. There had to be something she could do to make him press her back into the mattress, ignoring her protests...

She shook herself and forced her mind back to the actual question she needed to ask.

"Is there something I should ask? Fiona, I mean. Or try to find out from her?"

Damian looked her up or down. From the way his eyes lingered on the V of her pajama pants, she wondered if he was thinking about shoving her down and fucking her face, or something similar. She saw him stiffen in his shorts, just a little, and it was almost more than she could take. She told herself that it was only about keeping him happy, about surviving, and she knew that she was lying to herself.

"Find out what you can about her father—if he's been up to anything shady, how she feels about him. Stuff like that." He shook his head slowly. "I'm not sure she'll be able to give me much, or enough, but it's worth a try. And you'll get more than I can either way."

It didn't seem like information that would be useful, but hey, she wasn't the superspy assassin, so who was she to judge?

"Okay," she said.

Piper picked out a light sundress, then went into the bathroom to brush her teeth and put on some makeup. She had slept in too long to do her hair so a simple ponytail would have to do.

When she came out of the bathroom, Damian was nowhere to be seen. She was a little surprised by that, and maybe a bit sad. She had wondered what sort of face he'd make, seeing her dressed like this—

just a little playful, and her makeup done properly instead of in a hurry. Would he look her over like a utilitarian object, or would there be more there?

*You're not looking for more, Piper, cut this shit out. He's a kidnapper for God's sake!*

She shook her head and left the bedroom. Damian was out in the main suite. He had put on some slacks, which was good because another look at that tight ass would have undone her. He had not put on a shirt, however, and he was drinking black coffee as he scrolled through something on his phone. She could have tried to catch his attention before she left, but what was the point? He wasn't looking at her, and she wasn't supposed to want him to look at her.

She grabbed the clutch purse that matched the dress and headed out.

∼

The "little cafe" that Fiona had described was bigger than Piper's entire apartment. She took a seat at a small table that faced the front of the boat. She could mostly see the ocean from there, and less of the big white cruise ship beneath her. That seemed infinitely more pleasant.

She had never been out on the ocean before. She'd been on boats, once or twice, but mostly boats that were still docked, and to watch fireworks or something like that. Sailing out to the sea, where the coastline was barely visible... that was new to her, and she wasn't entirely sure why she was doing it. Well, she hadn't made the choice after all. And, given how things were going so far, it wasn't something she ever wanted to do again. Though there was obviously a certain bias involved.

Fiona didn't arrive until close to 9:30 AM. In a way, Piper was glad that the other woman was fashionably late. It gave her time to enjoy the first cup of coffee and stare out at the water. There was something truly incredible about not being able to see land, no matter how closely she looked. Her stomach tightened up into a knot over it—and then loosened into a gorgeous, free space that she'd never felt before.

When she then saw Fiona standing at the edge of the table, she jumped just a little.

"Oh, I'm sorry. I didn't realize you were there."

Fiona laughed. "Don't worry about it. Is this the first time you've been out here?"

"Yeah, I haven't had time to come up here yet. It's a nice spot. Good coffee."

Fiona shook her head as she sat down. "No, I mean is this the first time you've been out on the ocean?"

Piper nodded. "I mean, I've been out on the water before, but never like this. Not on a—" She caught herself and tried to look like someone who was ridiculously wealthy, spent time with people like Rich Chamberlain and his family, and had been on a yacht before.

Fiona's face grew serious, all of a sudden. "I'll order a coffee and something to eat for us. We need to talk."

A tight feeling clenched Piper's stomach again. She tried to keep the nervousness from spreading to her face, but that wasn't easy. She swallowed hard, matched Fiona's neutral expression, and nodded.

They got a French press full of coffee, a pot of cream and a cup of actual sugar cubes, as well as a plate of scones and mini muffins that were still hot. *It is absolutely ridiculous*, Piper thought to herself. There was no way any person could eat this much food, and she wasn't even sure that the two of them would make a dent. But, hey, at least she didn't have to worry that she was taking the only chocolate chip scone. She picked it up, cut it open, and smeared butter on the soft inside. *Probably only filthy peasants eat scones this way*—but she suddenly didn't care. She was hungry, and if there was food, well, when in Rome...

"So you've never been on a yacht like this before?" Fiona asked.

Piper shook her head. "No, I've never had the chance."

"What do you think of it?"

"It's gorgeous." The scone was so soft and fresh that she didn't even have to slug it down with coffee. *Absolutely incredible.* "When you're on the beach, you know, it seems like the water goes on forever, but then once you're on the water—My God, it really does go on forever."

"The planet's almost 75 percent water after all," Fiona said. Her eyes were drifting, wandering the horizon as she picked at her muffin. "So I guess it may as well go on forever."

Piper watched her, trying to think of what information might be useful to Damian, and how in the world she was going to get it for him. "*Hey, when is a good time to murder your dad?*" wasn't exactly the kind of question that would fly. But she didn't know this girl, and she didn't know what to do or say.

*So get to know her, doofus.*

"I can't believe how long it's been since school," Piper said, hoping her bullshit voice had held up over the years. "What have you been up to?"

Fiona made a snorting sound that did not sound like it belonged to someone who could probably buy several big islands. "Please, don't do that." She looked around, and when she was sure no one was nearby, she continued. "We didn't go to school together?"

"We didn't?" Piper asked like an absolute idiot. As soon as the words were out of her mouth, she winced.

"Of course we didn't. No offense, but I was a party girl when I was in college, but I wasn't so out of it that I forgot who I lived with for a year. I went along with it because I wasn't sure what was going on. At first, I thought your boyfriend must be one of Alex's friends, and I'd just misheard you. But then Alex started asking if we'd been friends, and I realized that couldn't be true."

Piper's heart felt like it was in her throat. She was obviously new at this whole murder-assassin thing, but if Fiona had told Alex that Piper wasn't an old friend, she had enough sense to know that she and Damian could be in a lot of trouble.

"So what did you tell him?"

Fiona offered a small smile. "I didn't tell him anything. I know Daddy hired plenty of private security for the boat because I can't leave my suite without bumping into someone with a clear earpiece. But Alex knows all of them. So I figure you and your 'boyfriend' are some kind of security that is supposed to be flying under the radar. That Alex doesn't know about. Something like that, right?"

It took Piper a second to realize that this was a request for confirmation, and she nodded.

"Yes," she said, hating that she was getting better at lying every day. "Something exactly like that."

Fiona nodded, clearly pleased with herself. "That's just like Daddy." She sighed. "I know he thinks Alex is just after the money..." She trailed off, staring out across the water.

"And what do you think?" Piper prompted.

It felt like way too much of a reach and a risk, asking the young bride to confide in her, but at the same time, Fiona had invited her up here, not one of her bridesmaids or theoretical friends. Her. There had to be some reason that she was seeking this sort of connection.

Fiona kept staring, and she was quiet for a long time.

"My mom left when I was a little girl," she said after a while. Her voice had the quiet, level tone that some people got when they were speaking about something deeply traumatic. Something they had processed and mostly put behind them—*mostly*. "She and Daddy had a big fight, I don't know what about exactly, but after that... she was gone. I found out that she'd died when I was in my late teens— that revelation was probably why I spent so much of my college years praying to the 'porcelain goddess'." Fiona gave another big sigh. "I never missed her exactly, not until we started planning the wedding. A girl's mother should be at her wedding, you know?"

Piper's familial relations had never been good, and she was pretty sure that if she ever found someone to marry, after all the bullshit she had gone through trying to get away from Todd, she was going to elope, or have a courthouse wedding or—literally anything else other than having a big fancy wedding. On a big, fancy yacht. As if she could afford any of this anyway.

"I get it," she said, to keep the girl talking.

"Alex was there, of course, and Daddy. Everyone kept telling me that I could have whatever I wanted." Fiona laughed, and the sound was strangely flat on the open air. "I picked the most ridiculous things just to see if someone would tell me no. And no one did. Of course, I don't think it would have been like that if Daddy weren't—" She shook her head hard. "It doesn't matter. We're out here now. And I'm married to Alex."

"What about the money?" It felt incredibly rude to press, but at the same time, Fiona had brought it up.

Fiona shrugged. "He signed the prenup. It's watertight." She narrowed her eyes at Piper. "You're not some sort of fiduciary or something, are you? You're too pretty and too interesting to be stuck with a job like that."

Piper laughed. "I know some very nice accountants." Which was true-ish.

"Nice, sure. But interesting?"

Piper laughed and shrugged.

Fiona got quiet again after a moment.

"I don't know. The thing about growing up with a ridiculous amount of money—or at least, with a father who has a ridiculous amount of money, no matter how much of it you can actually use or not—is that it starts to be hard to tell who's around because of the money and who's around because of you." Fiona groaned and put her head in her hands. "It's such stupid 'poor little rich girl' stuff to complain about. But does Alex really love me? Does it really matter?" She shook her head. "I don't know. How would I tell?"

Piper took a chance, reaching out and touching the back of Fiona's hand with her fingertips. "I think it matters. I think it must be really hard to have that doubt always in your head."

Fiona smiled, but to Piper, it looked like the too-bright smile of someone who has realized that she's been caught showing her emotions in public, and who now wants to change the topic.

"So, can you tell me more about your job? Or that cute guy on your arm? It seems like the two of you are more than just professional..."

Piper bit back the panic and tried to keep it off her face. "I mean, really, I'm potentially compromising things just by being here."

That sounded like something that a private security person would say. *Maybe?*

"And the guy? Damian is his name, right?"

Piper felt her cheeks flare with heat.

Fiona laughed in the most ungraceful way and stopped just short of pointing at Piper. It was the most genuine expression Piper thought she'd seen from the woman yet.

"Oh, oh, I see. You've been screwing the whole time, haven't you?"

"It's not like that..." Piper trailed off. She couldn't muster any kind of disagreement, not really.

Fiona shook her head. "Of course it is." She paused. "Look, everyone on this boat is pretending to be something. You and Damian are pretending to be guests, all my bridesmaids are pretending to know me inside and out, my father—" She faltered. "If we're all pretending, perhaps you could pretend to be my friend?"

Piper's heart ached. "Of course I can."

She wasn't even sure it would be pretending. Fiona seemed like such a nice girl. Something deep inside of her had been dinged up and damaged, yes, but nice. Kind. *Yeah...* Piper could be her friend.

She reached across and took Fiona's hand, giving it a hard squeeze.

*Easy as that*, part of her thought in a voice that sounded way too much like Damian's. *Easy as that.*

# 15

Three weeks passed on the boat, and they were the most luxurious weeks Piper had ever experienced in her life. Every night there was a fancy dinner with the kind of food she had only ever seen on TV cooking shows. Rack of lamb, scallops, swordfish, tuna, that weird geoduck thing that looked like a giant dick, prime cuts of beef, chicken cooked to perfection in extravagant sauces... Everything was rich, lovely, and delicious.

It turned out that being Fiona's friend came with a lot of perks that Piper hadn't anticipated. It sounded shitty, but she could see why other girls had flocked to try and be in Fiona's circle. Fiona wasn't exactly irresponsible with her money as she was fully aware that she had more of it than she could spend in a lifetime, and so she saw no need to hoard it.

The yacht was making a tour of the Caribbean islands, and Fiona went ashore every chance she got. She took Piper with her, and they just explored the bazaars and everything else that was set up to make a living off the American tourists who had stolen everything the islands had to offer and then tried to sell it back to them at a profit.

But Fiona didn't stick to the beaten tourist paths. Somehow, she always got someone to tell her where to go for a real meal and local market—the unfiltered truth. She bought as much as she could carry, which meant that she bought a lot of stuff.

"The least I can do is this," Fiona had said, gesturing at the piles of souvenirs. "I can't fix everything we've all done wrong here, but I can at least try and give them what I can. The kind of charity I can do physically on the islands would be bullshit, and I can't fix the systematic problems singlehandedly, but I can do this—give them the money I have."

That said, Piper saw plenty of plain money change hands. *It seemed to be why she was seeking out the local people,* Piper realized. Fiona gave a man money to purchase supplies and rebuild most of a community that had been devastated by a hurricane, and a young woman enough money to get to the mainland on the next ship so that she could rejoin her family. She just... gave.

*If Fiona were a character in a movie,* Piper thought, *she would be too good to be true.* Instead, she was just the kind of good that made you want to be better.

The first time Piper was sick, they'd been in Fiona's suite, surveying the various purchases Fiona had made with Fiona divvying up what she intended to keep, what she thought some of the other girls traveling with her might want, and what was going to be Piper's. Fiona gave her a sideways hug that somehow turned Piper towards her. Piper had been a little sick all day. They'd had breakfast off the ship, and given the state of water after the horrible hurricanes in the area the past several years, she had assumed that she'd just eaten something off. But during the hug, Piper's nausea peaked, and there was no controlling what happened next; she was about to be violently sick.

She clapped her hand over her mouth as the first heave happened, trying to keep it down as she bolted for the bathroom. She couldn't help remembering the way she had been sick just after she'd come aboard; the thought made it worse, and this time she didn't make it all the way to the toilet before she vomited.

The splat of the sick on the floor made her heave harder, and she struggled to get the toilet seat up and her head over the bowl before she was sick again. Her knees were shaking but damned if she was going to kneel in her vomit.

"Here," Fiona said gently behind her and shoved across a small footstool behind Piper.

Piper managed to sit before the next wave hit her and she gagged into the toilet again. Tears streamed down her cheeks at the intensity of it, and as the illness passed, she felt a different kind of sick. Even in her college days, she had never thrown up on a goddamn floor, not when she was blackout drunk and needed to be carried home. This was a kind of sick she'd never experienced.

Fiona rubbed a hand over her back; she was sitting on the edge of the bathtub, safe from the mess. Piper sat back a little, flushing the toilet and surveying the damage.

"Oh, don't worry about it," Fiona said. "We'll call someone to come and clean up, then get you sorted out in Alex's room. Hey, we got you plenty of new clothes from the bazaars."

Piper's stomach flipped, and she gagged again, but she had emptied her stomach, and there was nothing left to come out. The pressure on her back didn't let up.

"Are you sure Alex won't mind?"

Something dark crossed Fiona's face. "He'd damn well better not. Or if he does, he'd better keep his mouth shut about it."

Something occurred to Piper then. The time that Fiona was spending with her was really time that Fiona ought to have been spending with her new husband. Instead, the two didn't seem to be spending any time together at all. Well, maybe at night. Piper went back to Damian's cabin every night, and he still seemed to take a vicious delight in using her body mercilessly. It was nothing less than he had promised her after all, and God knew she was getting off on it—sometimes more than once a night.

Some nights he was fully present, murmuring her name as he fucked her, twisting her clit between his fingers and scraping his teeth over her nipples. Other nights he was far away somewhere, his gaze cold and distant. He was harsher then, more brutal.

It was hard to tell which nights she got off harder.

Maybe Fiona and Alex had been together so long that this honeymoon period didn't feel like anything special. Fiona had insinuated that the marriage wasn't entirely a love match; maybe they didn't particularly want to spend a lot of time together. Or maybe it was simply that they didn't like each other. But the darkness in Fiona's voice now was much harsher than before.

Piper nodded her okay. What the hell else was she going to do? She stood up and, with Fiona's help, cleaned herself off with a towel the best she could. She could smell the sick on her hair and her clothes, but it would get her across the hall without making more of a mess.

They picked their way out of the room, then Fiona grabbed an outfit off the bed. She sent a text as she led Piper across the hall to Alex's room. She didn't bother knocking.

Piper was so busy wondering for the first time why Alex and Fiona had completely separate suites, not even adjoining, that she didn't notice that she and Fiona had completely interrupted some kind of argument that was happening between Alex and his best man. She couldn't remember the guy's name.

"It has to get done," Alex was saying, his voice sharp. "You know this. It has to be done before we get back—"

"I'm working on it," the other man—Chris, that was it—said. "I told you; I have this handled."

"I'm starting to think this is why your services were such cut-throat prices." Alex started laughing. "Cutthroat, that's pretty great."

Fiona cleared her throat, and both of the men spun towards her. They flashed bright grins so shiny that they could have modeled for toothpaste commercials.

"Hi, honey," Alex said, but there was no emotion in his voice—happy or otherwise. "I didn't realize you'd come over tonight."

That was the weirdest thing Piper had ever heard. Even Damian wouldn't have greeted her like that; Piper was sure of it.

"We need to use your bathroom," Fiona said, her voice cold. "Mine is being cleaned."

"Of course. Chris is just leaving." Alex gave his "best man" a glare and jerked his head towards the door.

Chris scowled but nodded and left, pushing past Fiona—not entirely gently.

Fiona's expression darkened more, but Piper felt her own attention narrowing; she was starting to think she was going to be sick again.

"Fi..." she said quietly, trying to control her rebellious stomach.

"This way," Fiona said, taking Piper's hand and leading her through the suite. It was a bit silly; the suite was laid out like Fiona's except in reverse. "We'll need some privacy," she added, but she didn't bother looking in Alex's direction as she said it.

He made a *huffing* noise, and Piper heard the suite door close again—but by then, she was running again. At least this time she made it to the toilet. Fiona held her hair back. There wasn't anything in her stomach that could come up, but that didn't stop her body from trying to get rid of everything it could.

When the heaving stopped, she sagged against the side of the tub. Fiona was sitting up on the vanity now, watching her friend with a sad sort of concern.

"Sorry," Piper managed. "Just let me get cleaned up, and I'll get out of your way. I must have eaten something bad. I don't want you to have to take care of me."

"Please don't," Fiona said, glancing out the door at her new husband's suite. "At least, not until I can get back into my room. I don't... want to be here by myself."

It seemed like a strange request, but then, nothing about the last three or so weeks had been normal. Piper was pretty sure her stomach was as settled as it was going to be—at least for the moment.

She stood up slowly and started stripping off her clothes. She had stopped worrying about being naked in front of Fiona somewhere around the time the other woman had started grabbing Piper and spinning her like a doll to see how various things would fit on her. They were like sisters or best friends.

Piper felt a small twinge of regret, thinking of Marissa. She had no idea what was happening at home. Marissa had no idea what had happened. After all, it wasn't like Todd was going to stop by and say "Hey, kidnapped your best friend and sent her off with a murderer, she'll be back if he doesn't rape her to death."

Piper could wash her hands and face, but her hair was disgusting. There wasn't going to be anything for that but to have a shower.

"Do you mind?" she asked, gesturing towards the shower stall.

"Of course not," Fiona said. "Did you notice your bra doesn't fit anymore?"

Piper blinked hard and glanced down. She hadn't noticed, not really, though she'd noticed that when Damian twisted or sucked her nipples, they ached more than before. She had thought it was just arousal. But when she looked down...

*Yeah, my boobs are definitely spilling out of the cups.*

Not enough to look awful, but definitely enough to look like she was, well, a porn star.

"I... hadn't. Huh." Piper thought for a second. Her pants still fit, so she didn't think she'd put on weight...

Fiona rolled her eyes. "Get in the shower, Piper. We'll talk after."

Fiona stepped out of the room, and Piper spent a minute trying to figure out what in hell was happening. And then she noticed how rank her hair was and decided that everything else could wait until she was clean again.

～

Her hair washed and curly, and freshly dressed in the clothes that Fiona had left out for her, Piper stepped out into the main room. The suite had a seating area much like Fiona's. Fiona's, however, was furnished with delicate fabric settees and lounging couches; Alex's had high-backed back leather chairs. Fiona looked absolutely ridiculous in them; she was flowing softness, even when she wore a business expression; these chairs were masculine and demanding.

*Though*, Piper thought to herself, *Alex would look just as ridiculous in them.*

"Sit," Fiona said, and Piper did. "Feeling better?"

Better wasn't quite the word, but she didn't think she was going to throw up again. Any time soon, at least.

"Some, yes. Thank you for making sure I could get cleaned up. It really helped. I don't know what I ate."

Fiona wore a tiny smile for just a second. "I'd like to ask you a blunt question, if you don't mind."

Piper was surprised by the formality of Fiona's tone; she hadn't spoken like that since they'd had their first conversation up at the cafe.

"It's fine."

"You and your 'protection man'. You've been sleeping with him since you got on the boat, yes?"

Piper was long past the point of blushing about it. Fiona had asked a dozen different ways, but Piper had avoided answering. It had been pretty obvious for a very long time. But still... answering wasn't easy.

"Yes," she said. "Yes, we have."

"Mmm." Fiona nodded. "And exactly how much 'protection' has your 'protection man' been using?"

Piper opened her mouth to say of course they'd been careful, because she was always careful, and besides, she was on the pill... but neither of those things was true, even a little bit.

"Oh fuck," she said instead.

Fiona was quiet while Piper settled back into the awful, uncomfortable chair, trying to think of what to say, what to do. How could she even find out? Did they sell pregnancy tests onboard? She had meant to go to the yacht's shop anyway as she'd been expecting her period to start any day now, and kept being surprised that it hadn't.

"Do you think?" She couldn't bring herself to say the actual words, but Fiona clearly understood the question.

"I mean, it's definitely possible," she said, the strange formality slipping out of her tone. "You could have just eaten something awful, that's possible too. But... you're late, right? That's what you're thinking?"

Piper nodded.

A flash of what looked like pain crossed Fiona's face. "I have tests in my bathroom. We'll go back in just a few minutes."

It took several long beats before Piper could even guess at why Fiona was hurting. "You don't have any reason to use them?"

Fiona shook her head, her gaze turned away from Piper now. "I had hoped that this trip would be... That I could tell Daddy that it had happened. Before we got back to shore. But Alex..." Fiona sighed. "I was so sure it was something real. When Daddy made me sign that prenuptial agreement with him, I was so positive he was just being absurdly cautious. But now, after the way things have been since the ceremony..."

"What have things been like?" Fiona had hinted, here and there, but hadn't ever said it plainly. Piper wanted to hear what her friend had to say—and she would have been lying if she'd pretended that she didn't want to know what she could tell Damian.

Fiona sighed. "Alex hasn't so much as touched me since our wedding kiss. He was theoretically too drunk that night, but there's been... just nothing. Daddy kept saying it was all about the money for him, and I said I understood—I just hoped he was wrong. And he wasn't wrong." She forced a faint smile. "But hey. If you got knocked up on my honeymoon, at least someone has."

Piper watched as Fiona stood, walked over to Alex's wet bar, and poured herself three fingers of amber liquor. She did not offer anything to Piper, for which she was grateful.

After a few minutes, Fiona got a text message on her phone and nodded. "Come on." The sadness in her tone was so painful to hear.

Piper wasn't sure if hugging her friend would be helpful, or just make it worse. But focusing on Fiona's emotions was good. Better than thinking about her own—because that involved deciding what on God's green Earth she was going to do if she saw a plus sign instead of a minus. How did you tell a hired assassin that you were knocked up with his kid?

She followed Fiona into the other bathroom, then took the little plastic wrapped stick from Fiona when it was pressed into her hand.

"I'll give you some privacy," Fiona said before stepping out of the room and shutting the door.

Piper sat down on the edge of the tub. The cleaners had done a good job, and quickly; the room smelled clean and fresh, without any of that nasty air freshener crap people used. Just thinking about the artificial odor of one of those things made her stomach flip again, but she managed to keep it under control.

Right now, it was like Schrodinger's Pregnancy; it wasn't real until she took a test. She could be pregnant, or not pregnant.

But with Fiona's pointed comments, it was hard not to know for sure. There were other explanations, sure—lots of food could have made her gain weight, explaining the bra, food poisoning could explain the vomiting, and the late period could absolutely have been due to stress.

*But what was that thing about the razor?* The simplest solution was usually the right one. Which meant she needed to pee on the damn stick—preferably without getting her hand messy—and then find out what was going on.

How in the name of God could she possibly tell Damian if it was positive? Maybe there was nothing to tell him.

*One way to find out.*

Like a woman facing a firing squad, she sat down on the toilet, stuck the stick between her thighs, and peed.

The package instructions said to wait five minutes before trying to read the results, but the color in the window was already changing by the time she set the stick on the counter and cleaned herself. It was a clear plus by the time she picked it up and stared at it.

It was a strange sort of dissociation. She had no idea what to think regarding the results. They were clear and obvious; she was pregnant. She had heard plenty of times that there were false negatives on these things, but there were almost never false positives. So, unless she was some kind of miracle or statistical outlier, she was absolutely pregnant with Damian's child.

*Shit.* She was pretty sure she was going to be sick again.

Fiona knocked lightly and stepped into the bathroom. The stick was in full view on top of the vanity.

"So it's that," she said.

Piper leaned back, resting the back of her head on the edge of the bathtub. "Looks like."

"What are you going to do?" The question was somehow calm, kind and honest, instead of the scandalized query it could have been.

"I don't have a fucking idea." Piper shook her head and made herself sit up. "I have to tell him." She considered it. "Do I have to tell him?"

Fiona shrugged. "I'm the wrong person to ask, I think. How serious is it with you guys?"

"I don't think it'll last once we're off the boat."

*Truth.* She was pretty sure that she would be dropped off at the harbor with a suitcase full of clothes and a briefcase of money and no idea what to do next. She missed Marissa and missed her apartment, but how in the hell was she going to go back to just living her life, knowing Todd was out there? Knowing that this was something he'd been completely content to do to her? She wanted his blood—if only to make sure that hers was safe.

But no matter what she thought, Damian wasn't part of it.

Which hurt, in its own way. The sex was mind-blowingly incredible, but the past few weeks... there had been more than that. Conversations. He had asked about her time with Fiona, which she'd known he would do. But beyond that, he'd told her little bits and pieces of things. She knew he had been in the army first, then the CIA as a sniper. Then he had left and been private security for a while but got too itchy to stick it out. And now he was... *A freaking assassin!*

It wasn't ever all at once, and she definitely talked more than he did... but he was talking. And she liked the things he was saying. But would that last after this? Was she considering some kind of long-term relationship with a man who got literal blood on his hands and didn't think anything of it?

"No," she said clearer this time. "Definitely not."

Fiona nodded, and she didn't look particularly surprised. "So I'm clearly not the boss of you. And I know a lot of people would say that it's his kid and you have to tell him. But if... if you have no intentions of pursuing any kind of relationship, and you don't think you'll see him again..." She quickly glanced at Piper for apparent confirmation, and Piper nodded in agreement. "Then I don't see any point. I mean, if you feel obligated, of course, tell him. But otherwise... why do that to yourself?"

"I don't know," Piper said, more to herself than to Fiona.

"If you're worried about the financial aspect..." Fiona trailed off, and Piper looked straight at her. Fiona shrugged. "Everyone here wants something from me, but you're just here. You're the closest to a real friend I've ever had. I can help if you want help."

"I don't know what to do." It might have been the truest thing Piper had ever said in her life.

## 16

The next step was to check out the "best man's" suite, Damian had decided. He would have to make sure the guy was out, but he'd taken care of that easily enough. There were plenty of working girls on the ship happy to help a variety of sugar daddies not feel lonely while they were out at sea. He found a girl he trusted, handed her enough money for a week, and told her to keep the guy out of his cabin for a night. Simple.

He smiled to himself. Not every scam had to be complicated. That was where all the amateurs went wrong. If it weren't for the possible complication of another professional on board, he would have dealt with Chamberlain weeks ago, as soon as they entered international waters, stepped off onto one of the islands, and vanished into the mists.

He would have taken Piper with him because he promised, and he would have found a way to keep her safe. Maybe helped her and her friend that she was always talking about move to another city. Something. But he would have been gone.

Instead, he was looking over his shoulder and trying to figure out the right way to handle this. Which was, in and of itself, an amateur move. He needed to get this done. Before long, they would cross back into U.S. controlled space, and then he would actually be able to be charged for murder in a way that the courts could handle.

Well, assuming he was caught, which was a long assumption. But he didn't play the odds unless he knew that he would win.

He assembled the kit he wanted for the night—lockpicks, safe cracking tools (in case he needed to manage that sort of situation), *very* small demolition charges (in case his ear wasn't up to the job), a holdout pistol (which would do the job on someone if they were up close, but wouldn't go through a wall. It wouldn't even go through a body though really. Just something small, for emergencies), and his casual, semi-formal blacks, the ones that said "Oh, I just wandered down this hallway," without screaming the second half of that sentence: "to kill you."

He was about to head out when Piper came back to the cabin. There was something off about her, some hesitation in the way she walked. She hadn't moved like that since they had very first come aboard. Whatever strange relationship they had developed, they'd come to trust each other.

There was a different stirring in his stomach, one of worry. And, annoyingly, it wasn't about the job; it was about her. It had to be squashed, and fast, because even if this was his last job, she knew about the others. She knew about them, and she would never want anything else to do with him. She just wanted to be free of him. He'd seen that in her eyes, and more than once.

"Hey," he said because he needed to. "What's going on?"

She looked up at him, and for just a second, her eyes were completely open, hiding nothing. And then her expression closed again, her arms crossed tight over her midsection, and she looked away.

"I spent some time with Fiona and Alex today," she said. "Mostly with Fiona, but we had to—Anyway, we ran into Alex and Chris. And they were having a fight about something. Alex wants something done, and he's worried that Chris isn't doing it fast enough."

A shot of adrenaline ran through Damian; this confirmed that looking into Chris was the right move. It pushed away thoughts of the way Piper was holding herself, and the feelings it had caused at first. He grabbed her and pulled her close, kissing her hard.

"You're perfect," he said.

For the first kiss, she had been holding back somehow, but when he sealed his mouth over hers this time, she made a little noise in her throat and leaned into him, her tongue moving to tangle with his.

He was hard in a moment, and he wanted nothing more than to toss her on the bed and fuck her until she was screaming. But he had work to do. He ran his hand over her breast, digging into the bruises he'd left before, then running down and cupping her ass, pulling her against his hard cock.

"I have to go," he said, stepping away from her. He had to do it fast, or he wouldn't do it at all. "I have work to do. But I'll be back."

Piper looked up at him, her eyes blinking fast. Then she shook her head and forced herself to smile. "Okay. Yeah. That's great."

That strange feeling shook him again, and he paused. "Is everything okay?" He was missing something, and he had a strong feeling that it was important.

"No," Piper said, and that smile got a tiny amount more real. "I mean, yes. Everything's fine. You go—do whatever you need to do. I'll be here. I may go get dinner. Is that okay, for me to get dinner alone?"

Her manner was strange, and he was still worried. He took a long moment to take stock, but ultimately decided that no.

*No, there is nothing to do about any of it right now. Just keep going and see what happens next.*

If she had finally turned on him, there wouldn't be anything he could do about it.

∽

Crystal, the girl Damian had bought for the night, led Chris out of his room at exactly the time they had agreed. *Good girl.* He would tip her—if he got a chance.

One of the advantages to sneaking on to a ship under false pretenses to kill a billionaire philanthropist for crossing an organized crime family for several decades is that much like a hotel; the rooms were all basically the same layout. At least, they were under all the mess.

Chris' clothes were strewn about the room without a care, the bathroom was open and full of his toiletries—Damian swore he could see some sort of jasmine body wash in there—and a steamer trunk by his bed. This wasn't the 1920s, and he wasn't looking to start a new life in a new country. Jack was, but that was more of a wish fulfillment issue if he got out of this alive. Something was very, very wrong with this room.

A lot of somethings, actually. A search of the room revealed no go-bag, no suitcase, nothing hidden under the bed, or beneath the pillow. There was no way to pack up this junk quickly, no way to disappear. Not unless Chris threw it out the port window, and even that would take too much time.

Damian took a quick picture of the room, then threw a few dirty boxers and shirts off of the luggage. It was a new model with one of those rolling combination pins. He looked at the steamer trunk and frowned. He lifted it by its bottom and felt the weight of it more than the trunk itself. He took another picture of where the combination had been left. He intended to crack it but paused.

"There's no way that he's dumb enough..." he said out loud.

He saw the model number on the bottom and pulled out his phone, checking for the default combination on the manufacturer's website. Sure enough, when he entered 967, the trunk clicked open.

"You've got to be kidding me..."

While nothing incriminating was in plain sight, there was an obvious false bottom made of plywood hinged with some dollar store crap. Damian rolled his eyes and took another picture before pulling up the false bottom, revealing a 9mm pistol next to a detachable silencer, some ammo, a box of zip-ties from a hardware store, a large bottle of aspirin that he could only assume was used to create an overdose, and a note.

He lifted the pistol with his gloved hand and found that the serial number was still there instead of etched away. This wasn't just sloppy; it was amateurish, like a DIY assassination kit. He picked up the note, groaning a little. The handwriting was chicken scratch, but he was eventually able to decipher it.

*Tonight. 8PM. The Antique goes down – A.*

Code names, really? He shook his head, careful to put everything back exactly the way that it was according to the pictures. It was clear who had hired Chris now, but why did he hire someone in the first place? Why hire this amateur of all people?

In a way, it didn't matter. This was going to end tonight. Chamberlain, the assassins, Damian's life, everything he'd pretended wasn't real with Piper.

Everything.

# 17

Piper sat quietly in their room—no, her and Damian's room. It was best to start separating from him now, to keep herself distant. There was no 'us' with the two of them. Her and the baby, yes. She knew that she would keep it, that she'd love it unconditionally. She already did. But Damian? She didn't know how many people he had killed, how many people he hurt. She didn't know how deep the darkness that let him take a life really went.

So why did she feel, sitting on the bed, like she was a wife waiting for her husband to come home from war?

As she was laying back, her phone chimed with the custom alarm she had set for Fiona. She pulled it out and read.

*Piper, something's wrong, and I need a friend right away. No red alert, just come. Please. Please.*

She could hear the soft, plaintive voice in the text. Fiona wasn't asking for security; she needed someone to talk to. Piper rose immediately, making her way to Fiona's cabin with the longest strides she could make without risking slamming into someone. She knocked as a courtesy, then walked in to see Fiona shaking, a wine glass in her hand. A cursory glance showed that Fiona wasn't drunk, but her face was pale white and her eyes red from the tears streaking down her face. Her sleeveless dress showed marks on her shoulders. It took only a split second for Piper to lock the door behind her.

Fiona looked at her with wild-eyed fear, then settled after a moment. "Good. It's you. It's not him. Not him."

Piper walked over, arms open. Fiona sat the glass down and ran over to wrap her arms around her.

"Piper, he came in, he wouldn't stop, he didn't make any sense. I don't know what happened. He-he grabbed me." Her voice choked, and she sobbed against Piper's shoulder.

Carefully, Piper rubbed Fiona's back, whispering gentle words. "It's okay. I've got you. Where did your security go?"

Fiona laughed bitterly. "They left on my orders—stay out of the room in case things got heated in a good way. I'm an idiot. I could have been... Could have been..." She trailed off, her voice muffled against Piper's shoulder, the words no longer audible.

Piper listened quietly, just holding the poor girl. Fiona was the safest person on this ship, and she knew that, but telling her now wouldn't do any good. Not when she suspected that Damian had left to do something unspeakable to Fiona's father. She brushed Fiona's hair and felt the shaking slowly subside.

"You're not an idiot. Sometimes we expect better from people than who they really are. I'm not going anywhere, and Chris is not coming anywhere near you. He'd have to go through me." She smiled, filling her voice with a confidence she didn't really have. "And that's never going to happen. I promise."

Fiona nodded against her shoulder. The two stood there for a while, holding each other until Fiona had cried herself out. Piper could only think about the one she was foolish enough to trust, the bruises she'd asked for instead of ones inflicted on her. Were they really so different, Damian and Alex? She hoped not. She hoped that whatever Damian was, a part of him cared, a part of him thought of her as more than just a tool.

A grateful smile finally dawned on Fiona's face. There was no need for words. Piper helped her get to bed, her mind racing, her face as calming as she knew how to make it. Strong, confident, brave. All the things she didn't feel. All the things that Fiona needed.

When Fiona had started to relax beneath a blanket that cost more than some people's cars, Piper sat down on a chair partly facing the door and partly in Fiona's line of sight. A promise was a promise, no matter how scared she really was. Alex would have to get through her to get to Fiona. She wasn't pretending, not about her.

## 18

After all the time Damian had spent sneaking around the boat, working on getting the layout memorized and the routines of all the security lined up perfectly in his head, getting into Chamberlain's state suite was disgustingly easy. After this shit, he was definitely committed to the plan of becoming some dude who sold newspapers or hot dogs on a street corner. But if it weren't for that, he'd consider looking for work as a security advisor. After all, who better to protect you than the guy who used to try to kill you? He wasn't sure it would make a really superior business slogan though.

But after a moment, it was painfully obvious that this wasn't a case of him finding the perfect moment to slip through the glaringly obvious security gap that only occurred once every six hours. Someone had, yet again, gotten here before him. He saw a dark stain on the carpet that was clearly blood, and a chip in the wood next to the state door that had probably come from either a small caliber bullet or a blunt object being swung at a weird angle. He wasn't going to spend enough time staring at the damn thing to figure it out.

He heard a loud sound within the state suite, and he stopped worrying about what was going to happen next. Old military reflexes, the ones he'd honed to a fine edge overseas and then tightened still further in private security, kicked in. In one smooth motion, he drew his weapon and yanked the door open. The hinges were pointed towards him; if he had tried to kick it in, he probably would have broken his foot. He lucked out, however, since whoever was in the room hadn't locked it behind them.

The scene he saw in front of him was the strangest thing he had ever fucking seen. He took it in fast, just like his training had always forced him to do: Chamberlain, tied to a chair, with rope and amateur knots. A man—it only took Damian's brain a moment to recognize him as the best man at the wedding, with some incredibly white bread name. Chris.

Chris had a gun trained on Chamberlain, but his eyes were flicking wildly back and forth between the restrained man and—for fuck's sake—Alex, the newlywed, who was standing there with a gun trained on Chris.

"You can't do this to my father-in-law," Alex said in a voice that was so obviously rehearsed that Damian would have rolled his eyes if it wouldn't have taken his eyes off two weapons. He kept his own at his side, turning his body ever so slightly. It made him a narrower target and hid the weapon from these idiots. "I'll kill you myself."

Chamberlain seemed to be the only one who was bored as hell. "What is this, fucking amateur hour?"

Damian bristled just a little bit, but he didn't let it show. He was cold as ice now, everything but the killing drained out of him. The other two men, however—they both started shouting. It was a whole lot of bullshit; Alex screaming about how Chamberlain was going to sign some papers or he would call Fiona in to watch her old man die, while Chris screamed that he wasn't an amateur and if the son of a bitch said that again, Chris really would shoot him.

Damian kept his weapon steady at his side and waited for the situation to unfold. At this point, waiting was the best thing he could possibly do. And possibly, it was what made Chamberlain's eyes focus on him.

"You're not an amateur, are you, son?"

Damian's eyes narrowed at being called 'son', but there was something kind in the old man's tone that he couldn't bring himself to ignore all the way. It threatened to crack the ice, and that was dangerous. That couldn't be allowed to happen.

And also, to his annoyance, it caused the other two men to turn their focus to him. That was a problem. He pulled his weapon up, starting to draw on Alex—Chris was a wild card, and Damian was sure he could charge the idiot and knock him down before Chris could get an accurate shot off, but Alex moved like he'd at least gotten some practice in at the shooting range. Killed a man, maybe not, but he was at least familiar with a handgun.

Before he could zero in and pull the trigger, however, Chamberlain's voice snapped like a whip.

"No!" Damian knew the voice was for him. He glanced at the man as time slowed. "Him." He nodded towards Chris, and Damian made a split-second decision to follow the old man's lead.

He dropped to one knee to throw off any shot that Alex might have been about to make and put three silenced shots straight into the center mass of the target. There was a thump as the target collapsed.

A shot whizzed over Damian's head. It wasn't perfect, but he would have been clipped if he hadn't dropped. From the position on his knee, he leaped at Alex. He hit him at the knees like a linebacker, and the groom dropped hard and fast. His head cracked on the floor hard; he didn't go out, but he was dazed. Damian rolled him onto his front and put his knee in the other man's back. He grabbed the weapon and tossed it into the corner. No one was getting to it without going through him.

And he found himself glancing back at Chamberlain like he had, once upon his time, looked at his superiors. Waiting to hear the next instruction. This was who he had been in the military: ready to listen, ready to follow orders, and not under anyone else's control, but ready to take on whatever was necessary to make sure that his unit survived and his target did not. Including knowing which of those two missions was primary.

To his amusement, Chamberlain had shrugged out of the poorly tied ropes and was rubbing the circulation back into his arms.

"Idiots," he murmured. His gray suit was rumpled, but he looked better than a man in a hostage situation normally would. "Drag that fucker over here and tie him up, would you? I'm sure you know how to do it better than he did."

Without waiting for a response, Chamberlain looked over at the other target. *Chris*, Damian forced himself to think. *Another man*. If he was going to be a human being again, not just a killer, he had to start remembering that other people were... people. He would deal with the implications of his life later. Now, he just had to... do this right. *Baby steps*.

"Shame that fucking idiot didn't have the sense to die on a plastic tarp. Well, I imagine you'll know what to do about that after. Now, it's time we talk."

But before Chamberlain could say anything else, he seemed to lose his breath. He started to cough, and once he had one thick sounding huff out of his lungs, it seemed to take over his entire frame. It bent him over so hard that he dropped back onto the bed, still sitting—but it looked like, if the bed hadn't been there, he would have dropped to his knees.

Damian heaved Alex over his shoulder and carried him to the chair. He dropped the asshole into it and secured him with real knots that would actually hold up. The chair itself was way too rickety to hold up against someone determined, but since he was increasingly sure that Alex wasn't going to leave this room any more alive than his best man, he wasn't too worried about it. Not for now.

By the time he had Alex secure, Chamberlain's coughing fit had passed. He wiped his mouth with the back of his hand, and it came away bright red. Damian's eyes widened ever so slightly.

Chamberlain saw his gaze shift. The man nodded. "Sit down a minute. We'll talk, and then you can kill me. The Santiagos sent you?"

Damian didn't say anything, and Chamberlain stood slowly, making sure he had his legs under himself before he tried to walk, then gestured towards a pair of high-backed leather chairs that looked like they belonged in some kind of old-fashioned drawing room.

"Funny they sent you," Chamberlain said as he eased himself down into the seat. "Those bastards never could do their research. That was why it was always so easy to get in their way, block them from whatever crappy plan they had lined up next. Like dealing with mobsters from some bad Al Capone flick. Ridiculous."

Damian didn't exactly disagree, but he wasn't sure yet what the play was. Did Chamberlain have a gun located somewhere near these chairs? Was there a recording device he could use to expose Damian's irritation at the Santiagos, who had sent him on this absurd mission that was going to get him killed? Because he'd finally had to admit to himself—Todd played the dutiful son too well. Carlos was behind this, just as entwined as his stepson. Damian was supposed to die here. Whether it was a dastardly "he knows too much" situation, or a simple decision that he had outlived his usefulness somehow, the Santiagos expected to be done with him after this.

It took another long moment, and then he decided the best way to cast his lot.

"Can I get you anything? Water or something?" he asked, coming over to the chairs.

When Chamberlain shook his head, Damian let himself sink into the opposite chair.

"They sent me," Damian said.

And with those simple words, he cut his ties for good. If they were words he had uttered as he put a gun to Chamberlain's face, maybe it would have been something different, but that wasn't what was happening. Instead, he was making a confession.

Chamberlain nodded. Of course, this wasn't news to him. "What do they have on you?"

Damian shrugged. "It's a pretty typical story."

"Tell me anyway."

It only took a minute, really. He had meant it when he said it was typical. But Chamberlain listened like it was the first time he had ever heard of a man who'd risked everything for someone—and ended up paying everything. But throughout, Chamberlain was nodding along, agreeing to everything that Damian said. He asked a question or two about Damian's sister. Damian answered the questions about Alison carefully, nervous about revealing too much... but at the same time, he believed the instinct that told him this was his way out.

After Damian's story was complete, Chamberlain nodded again, his eyes focused on the middle distance. "Do you know why I say this is all irrelevant?"

Damian shook his head.

Chamberlain smiled, just a little. "There's no need to murder me. Cancer's going to take care of that in, hmm... three months or so, the doctors say. I think it'll be sooner than that, honestly." He shot a long look at Damian. "Maybe tonight."

Damian narrowed his eyes, considering the implications of what the man was saying. "Cancer?"

"Yes. It turns out that prostate cancer is very treatable when it's caught early. By the time it's metastasized into your lungs..." He shook his head. "Get your cancer screenings is my point."

"And what does that have to do with tonight?"

"You're going to deal with that." Chamberlain nodded in the direction of the body on the floor. "Then you're going to deal with my bastard son-in-law. And then you're going to take care of me, just like you said you would."

Damian couldn't choke back the laugh. "Are you arranging your murder, old man?"

He didn't quite mean to let the derogatory phrase slip out, but there was something he respected in this man that made it... seem right.

"Rich," Chamberlain said. "And no. I'm arranging my suicide."

## 19

It was a handful of minutes later, and Damian was alternating between splashing Alex's face with cold water and slapping his cheek to bring him back to his senses. After a moment, Alex was staring up at him blearily. It took a moment for the fear to sink back in.

"Hey," he said, trying to sit up more, and finding himself entirely restrained by his bonds. "Hey. I can explain all of this. Hey." His eyes were rolling around the room, and he found Chamberlain. "Let me go, please, Rich. Come on."

Chamberlain—Rich—laughed, setting off another coughing fit, although this one wasn't so bad. "You fucking idiot. You tried to have me killed."

"No," Alex said, shaking his head as hard as he could. He strained against the ropes but didn't get anywhere. "No, I wouldn't ever—this guy isn't mine—"

"I know that. He's an actual professional, and you couldn't afford him. But that bastard…" He nodded towards the body on the carpet, which Damian really had to deal with soon. Getting the blood out of the floor was going to be a complete pain in the ass already. "What did you do, hire him in the fucking classifieds?"

"Craigslist," Damian informed him, out of the side of his mouth.

He had stepped back, and his weapon was ready, but he was confident about Alex's restraints, and Rich had the sense to stay safely out of range.

Alex glared at Damian in a way that made it incredibly obvious that Damian was correct.

"Look," Alex said. "I didn't mean for him to—I just wanted to make sure that—"

There wasn't any explanation, and eventually, Alex sagged. Maybe he thought the truth would save him, or maybe he knew what was coming and didn't want the weight on his soul.

"I hired him, yeah. I knew what was coming for you." He nodded at Damian. "And if someone was going to take you out, I wanted it to be me, not the Santiagos. I wanted to show them that I was a threat so they wouldn't challenge the business, once it was mine."

Rich shook his head. "You didn't even read the prenup. It's not yours. It'll never be yours. It all belongs to Fiona."

Alex started to curse, but before he could build up a real head of steam, he started to cry.

"The thing is, you stupid prick, I had him researched before I let him on my ship. I found out that you met him in a bar just a month ago. He told you he was a contract killer, didn't he?"

Alex nodded in such a pathetic way that Damian had to cover his mouth to keep from smiling where the stupid jackass would see.

"He was a dog walker, you idiot. Sometimes a food delivery guy. He told you he could kill me because he thought, huh, how hard could it be?" Rich shot a long look at Damian, then nodded. "How hard can it be, son?"

This time, they had prepped for it to be done clean. When Damian shot the man this time, there was a plastic tarp ready for the blood. Alex gasped a few times, trying to breathe, and then his head hung down. He was dead, his body just took a few minutes to get the message. It was like that sometimes.

"You understand from here?"

Damian nodded. "You want me to make it look like he's the one who killed you. Like you shot him. Get rid of the other body. Simple, really."

Rich nodded. Something was gone from his body now, some vitality that he'd had since Damian had walked into the room an hour ago. He looked old. Not just tired and sick, but old.

"Do you—Should I get your daughter? Give her a chance to say goodbye?"

Rich shook his head, a slow side to side movement that made Damian's stomach clench. He hoped that, however he died, it wouldn't be like this. Torn up by something that had stolen away every bit of hope he'd ever had.

"She knows it'll be soon. That's why we took this cruise. It was the best way she could think of to spend time with me at the end. She's been here every day. She'll be here when it matters."

There was enough mercenary left in Damian to make him ask another question. "And what about me? What guarantee do I have that she'll follow through on your offer and buy my contract out from the Santiagos?"

He shook his head. "Give me just a minute." He pulled out a phone and tapped a bunch of keys, clicked apps open, and sent messages.

"There. Through all the secure channels. It'll be taken care of by morning. I assume you have identities that those bastards don't know about?"

"Yes."

"Then that will be enough for them to steer clear of you. I've let them know you're untouchable, or all the proof I've been gathering of their criminal activities will go to the federal authorities—and they haven't had enough money to buy out the feds yet. Disappear—take that pretty girl of yours with you."

"I will."

"And." Now the man looked old and sad, and again Damian hoped he would never look like this in his life. "If you get the chance, look in on Fiona now and then. Make sure she's well. This will hit her harder than she'll realize at first." Rich gave a long sigh. "I've noticed that she and your girl are becoming good friends. If you can find a safe way for them to keep in touch?"

"I'll try."

"Thank you." Rich stopped for a moment, a bemused look crossing his face. "Damian, are you a religious man?"

It was always the old men who started telling tales before death. Damian had long since learned to humor them.

"Not since I was young." Damian rubbed his hands together without thinking, like he was washing them in the sink. "And very different."

"I can understand that. Religion has certain obligations that are difficult to respect. But I have never met a man who didn't have something on their conscience. Something that they could ask forgiveness for, or just say because they need to get the words out of their head." Chamberlain sat on the bed, nodding to the chair. "Sit, please."

Damian knew that they had time. Chamberlain was too calm, too collected for it to be any other way. There was a risk that this was a stall tactic, but false sincerity was something he had learned to identify. He'd heard, 'I have a family' more times than he could count. So, he sat and listened to the old man.

"Damian, I am the one person in the world who can listen to anything you have to say and can tell you honestly that I'll never repeat it to another living soul—since the window of time to betray your confidence is something like thirty minutes." He cracked a grin. "The dead, then I might tell, but I don't think they'll bother you any." Despite himself, Damian laughed at the ghoulish joke that could only come from a man who had long accepted his fate. "And I know when a man needs to get something off his chest."

Damian smiled at the old man. It really was a shame to kill him. A shame he was dying at all. "You might be right." It was a quiet thing, his voice as he spoke. He kept his eyes on Chamberlain; his body language, his face, was laid bare to a man whose time left could be counted in minutes. "It's about a girl."

Rich murmured, "Isn't it always?"

This time he didn't ask if Damian wanted anything to drink. He reached over to a cart that had been rolled close to the bed. He pulled out two glasses and a bottle of whiskey, and Damian had to keep himself from laughing. The old man had probably enjoyed a nice drink before bed. And then he sobered; it might very well be to try and deal with the pain.

Rich poured a single finger of whiskey for Damian, and three for himself. "I won't bore you with the details, but this stuff makes me look young. And I don't know about you, but when a woman's involved, I've always found it easier with a bit of liquor."

Damian couldn't argue with that; he took a sip of the whiskey, enjoying the warmth of it. He wasn't a hard drinker—too easy to cloud his mind at the wrong moment—but he knew enough to know this was too expensive for his palate. The man wasn't wrong.

"Her name is Piper. I was tricked—didn't do my research either, as you can see." Rich chuckled, drinking a bit more liberally. "She wasn't meant to be here at all. Not a thing to do with this. Honestly, if she weren't here, she'd be sitting in front of a laptop. She's a bit like you actually. She does crowdfunding work—helping people with ideas to make them real. Now, instead, she's part of a bloody business that—I was told that there would be a girl, but that she'd be different. Hardened to this. But Piper's strong, I'll give her that." He downed a bit more of the whiskey. "But I came in and changed her. She can't be who she was. She can go back, sure, but..." He trailed off, looking down at the glass.

"But she saw the other side." Damian looked up and saw a level of understanding that was rare in a civilian. "Don't be surprised. Once Fiona started noticing that bodyguards were always around her, I had to ease her into the idea that one day, people would try to kill her. Doesn't matter if someone's thirteen or twenty-two, no one should have to hear that. But we tell them. We have to because we are who we are."

Damian looked at him with an intensity he hadn't felt in quite some time—a hell of a thing considering two men were dead by his hand. "And who am I?"

Chamberlain, of all things, laughed. "You're asking me?"

"You're the one with some psych classes and a few decades of experience. I figured you might have some idea."

"A potshot at a dying man about how old he is? That's a low blow, son." He furrowed his brow. "Truth is, I think you're a man fighting a war on two fronts. The Santiagos? Bah, that's nothing. No, you're fighting against every time you pulled the trigger, and every time you look at your girl and pretend the world was like it was when you were sixteen, and everything was full of hope and promise."

"I'm not fighting against it; I fought to do it."

"Ghosts, my boy, ghosts. How many of them do you remember? How many jobs? How many ways have you seen them die, and how many times have you seen the same one die when you close your eyes?"

Damian didn't say a word. He just gripped his glass tighter and took the whiskey as a shot.

"Yeah, that sounds about right." Chamberlain refilled his glass, even more generously this time. "You can't change what you did. None of us can. Alex? He's dead and gone. He's a fucking idiot—or was—but even if he'd gotten a kick in the ass in the right direction, it wouldn't stop the fact that he'd been a fucking idiot his whole life."

Damian snorted. "You should give seminars."

"I do."

"Smartass. So what, I am who I am because of all that I've done? That's it, that's the end?"

"That girl of yours. You're not happy with how you treated her? I'm not stupid, that's a rhetorical question. I can see it just fine on your face anyway. Yes. You've done unspeakable things. You probably hurt her too." Chamberlain took a large pull of his drink, then noticed that Damian's was mysteriously empty and poured some more for both of them. "Ask yourself this. How much do you think you're gonna hurt her tomorrow?"

Damian was quiet for a moment. He put his finger in the whiskey, swirling it gently. It probably broke a few hundred rules on how to properly drink the stuff, but proper wasn't ever his deal. "I honestly don't know."

"Then make the decision. Make the decision because you are who you are, because it's what you've decided. Not what I say. Not what the Santiagos say. Not what the service said. Not even what the lady says. It's you, Damian. It always was."

The two men finished their drinks in silence. The truth was too sharp and ringing to be broken by more words, and both of them knew it. The minutes ticked by, agonizingly slowly. Damian felt himself more and more drawn to put a stop to all of this, but there was no way out. Chamberlain was right. But this was his last job, one way or another.

Finally, the old man sighed. "I'm ready, Damian." He laid back, whether by choice or by need, Damian would never know.

Chamberlain's head was sunk into the plush pillow, the sheets that were probably a thousand thread count or something ridiculous turned down on the bed. "Can you—if it's possible? I'd rather it didn't hurt. Maybe it sounds weak, but everything has hurt so much the past few weeks..."

"It won't hurt," Damian said. He reached into the small pouch he kept inside his pants leg and removed a vial and a covered syringe. "Close your eyes."

The old man did, and Damian injected him just under the fingernail. The man winced, but it was just a few moments before his body went slack. Once the anesthetic had taken hold, that was when Damian administered the poison.

It would be untraceable just hours after the body was dead, but between then and now, it was a dangerous window. He couldn't allow suspicion to fall on him.

And beyond that, what it did to the body—it wasn't pretty. If he hadn't started with the anesthetic, his claim that none of it would hurt would have been a lie. As the body thrashed, trying to desperately to stay alive even as it was killing itself from the inside out, Damian held the hand of the only man who had ever tried to keep him alive.

When it was done, he arranged all the bodies the way they would need to be. He disposed of the idiot amateur simply enough—tossing him overboard the way he had always planned to do with another body. And then, when he knew the toxin would be clear, and everything was properly arranged, he fired two shots from Alex's gun.

He left through the panic room door before the smoke had cleared, and before the rest of Rich's security force could enter the room.

## 20

By the time Piper heard the gunshots, Fiona had curled up with her head in her lap, having cried herself to sleep. Piper was stroking the other woman's hair and wondering when was the last time she'd been properly mothered. But the two shots, loud and strident, made her jump. Her jump jostled Fiona enough that she jolted upright.

"What was that?" she asked, rubbing the sleep out of her eyes.

"I don't think we should go," Piper said.

Her stomach was twisted into knots. She knew what those sounds meant. Either Damian's work was done, or Damian was dead. Either way, she was going to fall apart soon. She thought of the tiny little one growing inside of her, the one she hadn't had a chance to tell Damian about yet. What if she never could? What if he'd finally run out of luck, and she never got the chance?

Fiona shook her head hard. She stood up, almost stumbled, and caught herself on the couch. "No. Piper, I think those were gunshots. I think Daddy—" She choked off the words.

Piper stood up and gripped the woman—her friend's—arm. "Fiona. If something's happened to your dad, the security team will handle it. And if they can't—we'll just get killed rushing in there and trying to save people who probably don't need to be saved."

Fiona jerked her arm free, and Piper winced. She had a terrible, terrible understanding of what Fiona was going to find, and she wanted to somehow protect her friend. But this was always what it was going to come down to, wasn't it? This had always been the real plan.

"Come with me or don't," Fiona said, clearly trying to mask her fear with bravado.

Piper came. They rushed down the hallway, crossing the short distance to Mr. Chamberlain's cabin. Piper was a little surprised not to see Fiona's new husband standing out there in the hallway with them—and then her stomach twisted farther. If he'd gotten in Damian's way... there would be nothing to be done. Damian had a job to do, and Alex wasn't going to get in the way. And there had been the suspicions that Alex was somehow involved... but Piper didn't want to think about that now. Not when Fiona was twisting the knob of an obviously locked door, then pounding on it, screaming for her father.

After a moment, someone in a suit with a visible clear earpiece moved her less than gently out of the way. He pulled out a key and unlocked the door, then pushed it open. He tried to get in first, probably to shout clear like they did in movies or something, but Fiona elbowed him out of the way. Which is why she saw the horror tableau first.

To Piper, knowing what had happened, it was all so obviously staged. Just pretend. She would ask Damian later what had really happened, and he would tell her. Or he'd lie. She didn't know which one. Right now, it didn't matter.

Alex's body was laid out on the floor, a pool of blood spreading from his torso. There were several gunshot wounds in his chest, and gunshot wounds didn't look small or delicate like they did in the movies. His chest was a disgusting mess. Piper felt the bile rise in her throat and had to choke back the urge to vomit.

Fiona was screaming on her knees because Rich Chamberlain had been shot as well. There was a matching pool of blood covering his mattress, which spilled onto the floor.

And no Damian.

Security rushed them back out of the room as quickly as they had gotten in; Piper helped a big linebacker of a guy lift Fiona out. *It won't make much of a difference*, Piper thought; the destruction of the room would already be stained indelibly in Fiona's mind. But they could at least keep her from staring at it.

The ship's doctor came and gave Fiona something to help her sleep, and after making sure that she was relaxed, Piper left the room. She passed another woman in the hall, one of the bridesmaids. She was tapping lightly at the door and then slipping inside, presumably to sit with Fiona until she woke up. Piper wanted to do more, but she was worn out. There was nothing left.

The ship was quiet, although everyone seemed to be gathered in the common areas. If news passed around a small town quickly, it probably passed around a glass bottle of a ship even faster. She was being stared at, gawked at even. She checked her hands and knees—no signs of blood. So just the news, then, that she'd seen what had happened.

She wondered what rumors were already flying around, and then worked hard to put them out of her mind. There was no point in thinking about it. It was already the worst that it could possibly be.

She made her way to her and Damian's cabin and wondered what she would find. *A man, covered in blood? That cold, killer look back in his eyes? That vicious sneer, those harsh hands which had somehow coaxed such incredible pleasure out of your body?*

She had no idea. She almost wished that he would be gone. Just a specter that had disappeared without a trace. An imaginary man she had used in her fantasies while she went out and found some nice, normal guy to marry.

Assuming she could find someone willing to deal with the baby in her belly.

She sighed. This was all absolutely shit. She had no idea what he would do if he found out. Should she even tell him? He didn't seem the sort to tenderly lay his hand over the lowest part of her belly and whisper that he'd always take care of both of them. Hell, maybe he would kill her too. She didn't know. She didn't know him.

She pushed the door open, completely split on whether or not she wanted to see Damian there. When she saw him sitting on the bed, though, his hands clasped together between his knees, she felt a surge of relief. She let the door swing shut behind her as she ran to him. He stood, clearly surprised, and only just managed to catch her as her weight slammed into him.

"Hey," he said, reaching up to stroke her hair as she pressed her face into her neck. She realized she was crying only when she felt the wetness on his skin. "Hey, Piper. Hey."

"Sorry," she mumbled, not understanding where the words were coming from, or even why. "I didn't mean to—I'm sorry."

He was rocking her gently back and forth. Had he been trained in this too, how to lure a woman into relaxation so that he could destroy her as needed? It seemed plausible. Why wouldn't someone need to do that? Get close and then end her. But it seemed like more of a move that a woman would need to pull.

She laughed a little to herself. Maybe if they got off this damn boat alive, he would end up training her to be an assassin too. She knew that what she'd witnessed wouldn't ever be as painful as what Fiona had seen, but it wouldn't ever leave her mind. She knew she would see those two corpses in her nightmares for the rest of her life. It was sickening and terrifying—and she'd always be afraid of it, as long as she lived.

"You saw the room?"

She nodded into his chest.

He sighed. "I'm sorry. I wish you hadn't seen that. It was... gruesome."

"You did all that?"

He tensed just a little, and she realized that it could sound like the kind of question a person might ask when they were wearing a wire or looking for verification of something before selling that information. Something... that she wouldn't ever do. *Strange.* She was fully aware that this wasn't anything in her head or in her heart. Whatever happened next with him, she wouldn't try to hurt him. It wasn't... right. It just didn't make sense.

"Yes," he said, and it took her a moment to remember the question.

She felt something rush out of him—something that felt soft and sad. And hard, at the same time. Suddenly, he was leaning into her just as much as she was leaning into him. It felt... peaceful somehow. She didn't understand it.

"Yes," he said again. "But that was the last time. He—Things were going on that I didn't realize. And I'm done with that life. He made sure of it. So I'm getting off this boat in two days, and I'm walking away from my life."

The soft warmth that had been washing through her at his words suddenly went cold.

"Oh," she said.

There was a long pause, and neither of them said anything.

"Were you... did you have something else in mind?" His voice was light and curious.

She thought of pulling back farther to see his face and then decided against it. What good would come of seeing how casually he was viewing this whole thing?

"No." She managed another little laugh and kept this one far away from hysteria. Which was good because she felt it looming there, ready to take her on and take her apart. Blurring into that space where laughing and crying were basically the same.

How could she possibly explain to him what had happened? After all, it had happened to her, hadn't it? Not really something that was his problem.

"No," she said again. She realized the heel of her hand was rubbing gently at her stomach and forced it to stop.

His face fell, and she understood. It had to feel awful to feel like someone was rejecting you because of your past. God, she knew how that felt, really. She stepped into him, going up on her tiptoes to press her lips against his. It only took a minute for him to respond, and when he did, his whole body came into her at once.

He crushed her against him, his arms wrapped tight around her, and she whimpered into his mouth. That evoked a snarl, and he was backing her up until her knees hit the bed, then pushing her down. She was wearing loose, relaxed pants and plain panties; they were gone in a moment.

She pulled off her shirt and worked the hooks on her bra, then tossed it aside. She pulled at the hem of his shirt and shoved it up and out of the way so that she could run her hands over the planes of his stomach and the hard expanse of his shoulders.

"Fuck me," she said, putting every ounce of eagerness into her voice.

He was already shucking his jeans and boxers, then heaved both of them farther up the bed. He stayed up on his knees and pulled her up to him, lining up his cock and then shoving in with one long thrust.

It hurt, it stung—not that it had ever stopped hurting with him, especially not at first—but when Piper cried out, it was because she wanted more. His cock drove into her at such a vicious angle in that position, and he was so hard, so achingly hard. Part of her wondered —was he always like this after? Did he always need a woman to fuck, someone to remind him that he was alive? Because before, he had only been this swollen, this close to splitting her open when he'd used the belt on her or tied her down. She felt his balls slapping against her ass, tight and ready, and knew he was holding back for her.

And then his thumb pressed down on her clit, moving in the tight up and down motion that she needed, that he'd learned over the past few weeks. She was crying out hard, clenching down on his cock at every thrust, her body soaring and soaring until the orgasm shattered over her. She clenched her teeth to keep from screaming, part of her brain knowing that a scream would bring people running for entirely the wrong reason.

She heard his low sounds as he let himself get close to the edge, her pleasure sated, and then felt the heavy pulse of his orgasm moving through him as his fingers tightened into her hips hard enough to leave marks. They sank down onto the bed together, his cock moving in her slowly as the last of his orgasm rolled through him, and her cunt pulsed against him. Soft and steady.

He shifted to the side so he wouldn't land on top of her, but instead of rolling to his back or immediately standing, as he had so often, he curled into her, his arm coming around her and tugging her close. It was so sweet it made her heart go soft.

Except he gripped her belly, and the soft movement there made her gag hard. She'd been so nauseated for days, and the pressure was more than she could stand. She knew she wasn't going to be able to hold it back, and if she spoke, she would be sick all over the bed. The only solution was to press the back of her hand to her mouth, scoot away from him as fast as she could, and flat out run towards the bathroom.

She barely made it; the first rush of vomit was coming before she could kneel over the toilet. She thanked whoever that the top of the seat was up, or she would have made a terrible mess. As it was, the water splashed everywhere, and the smell and the splash combined brought a fresh wave of sick over her.

In the pause between, she managed to get to her knees and grip the sides of the toilet, keeping her balance as the world spun. His cum was leaking down her thighs, and she told herself the tears on her cheeks were just from the violence of her sickness.

*Please don't let him put it together*, she begged as hard as she could. *Please. Please don't let him.*

Another wave of nausea passed over her, and she was sick again. She had no idea how a person could hold this much; she'd been sick over and over the past few days, barely able to eat or drink or anything, and yet, here she was.

He padded into the bathroom, and he moved loud enough so that she heard him. She didn't look at him, not yet. She was worried that her stomach would clench again, but she was also worried that he would look at her and see the truth, know that he'd put a baby in her belly and that she didn't know how to tell him about it.

"I'm sorry," he said quietly.

He brushed her hair back from her face and then wet a washcloth and handed it to her to wipe her mouth. His gaze was focused over her head, and his voice was flat, completely neutral.

"Look, I—I get it. I'll find somewhere else to be until the boat docks. And don't worry—I won't let anyone bother you because of this. I promise. And I'll get you the money. You deserve to be paid for—for what you've done here."

He stood up and walked out of the room. Piper tried to think of something to say to him, but what was there possibly to say?

*Please don't leave, Mr. Assassin. I'm pregnant with your lovechild, could you please stick around and—*

And what, raise a family? Settle down in some normal nine to five job and just ride a desk all day? Find a position with health insurance and paid sick leave?

*No. It's best to let him go.*

Let Damian walk out of her life so she could... figure out what to do next.

Piper put her head on her knees until she heard the door to the cabin close. Then she stood up, forced herself to get dressed in regular clothes, and went to bed. Damian had even straightened the sheets so that the evidence of their wild sex wasn't obvious. She couldn't think of anything else to do, and she was really and truly exhausted.

She pulled off her dirty clothes, curled up under the covers, and let herself drift off to sleep.

∼

When the boat docked, three days later, Piper hadn't seen Damian. She didn't know where he was staying; she didn't even know if he was still on the ship. She had seen plenty of Fiona; Piper had spent plenty of time in the other woman's company, consoling her as the loss of her father and brand-new husband had taken root. No one at all seemed particularly surprised that she was more heartbroken over the loss of her father than the man she'd married.

But it wasn't Fiona that Piper wanted every time she was sick to her stomach, or too tired to move, or on the day she realized that none of her bras fit anymore. She still didn't know what she was going to do. All of Damian's things had been moved out of the cabin one day while she was out with Fiona. After that happened, she realized that she had no real way to contact him or try to talk to him about being pregnant with his child. She had tried asking a few of the ship crew, but none of them knew anything. Whether he'd paid them or they truly had no idea, there was no way to know.

And without being able to tell him what was going on, all she could do was hope that she could make the right choice for herself. She should have stopped him before he left the cabin that night. She knew what he thought—that she had finally realized how much blood was on his hands and couldn't stand to have him touch her anymore. She should have told him the truth about that, at least, even if she couldn't bear to tell him about the rest. She shouldn't have let him think that she despised him or was that nauseated by him.

Before the boat docked, she said her goodbyes to Fiona. She made sure her new friend had her phone number and address, although Piper found herself doubting that she would ever really hear from Fiona Chamberlain again. Why would a newly married and widowed woman of society want anything to do with her?

But Fiona had promised to have all of Piper's things sent back to Piper's apartment, so she didn't have to worry about that. As Fiona said it, Piper suddenly found herself remembering those first moments in the back of the SUV, after Todd had grabbed her and tossed her in. The way he had watched her as he threatened her. She'd lived in these clothes for a month, and they made her skin itch and her stomach clench. Granted, that didn't take much at all these days.

"Don't worry about it," she'd told Fiona. "You can burn them for all I care."

As soon as they'd gotten close enough to the real world to have proper cell service, Piper had sent a single message from Fiona's phone. As soon as she walked down the gangplank, arms wrapped around her, and she was wrapped up in her best friend's embrace.

"I got you," Marissa said, her voice quiet. "We got this."

Piper squeezed back, the enormity of everything sinking in. She started to shake, and Marissa gently led her back to her car.

"It's okay," Marissa said as they got into the car, and Piper started to cry. "You're safe."

## 21

Damian watched Piper disembark through a pair of high-powered binoculars. He was high up in the crow's nest, the spot where he had first started to suspect there was someone else on board the ship who was going to make his life harder. He'd been in various places around the ship for the past few days. He had heard that Piper was trying to make inquiries, but no one was interested in bothering him.

The upset caused by Chamberlain's death had disrupted the ship's routine more than enough; there was nothing for him to worry about at this point. The ship's onboard security as well as Chamberlain's personal guards were all convinced that the attack had been part of Alex's attack on his newly-minted father-in-law. Since they were in international waters when the attack occurred, it was unlikely any further investigation would be necessary.

And, even if it were, Damian would be gone fast enough that it didn't matter.

But as he watched Piper fall into the arms of a dark-skinned woman on the dock, he found himself wondering—what if he didn't leave the country? What if he stayed here, got a regular job, and got in touch with Piper as a—well, a more honest man? What if he decided that he was going to clean up his act and his life and more?

There had been something between them. He would never be able to deny that. But he also couldn't forget the last night they'd been together. It had been incredible, something he'd never experienced. She was looking up at him with something that felt warm and soft—he didn't dare to call it love—and then the look had twisted.

She had scrambled out from under him, her hand pressed to her mouth, and she'd gotten so sick that he thought she might turn herself inside out. Like she had when they first came into the cabin, when she'd just been kidnapped and had no idea what was happening.

It made sense she would remember that now.

He pressed a button on his phone. It sent a chunk of money into an offshore account in her name. It was a pretty decent number, one with six zeroes. If she were careful, she would live the rest of her life and never work another day. Unless she wanted to. He didn't figure her for someone who would just stop working; she had too much push in her. Even if she didn't stick at some traditional job, she'd do charity work. Something like that. Her new friend Fiona would help her get started. If that was what she wanted to do.

There would be no place in her life for someone like him. He knew the nightmares wouldn't ever stop. He knew that the darkness that had driven him into this life would need to be dealt with. He wasn't stupid. She didn't need a haunted ghost in her space dragging her life down into nothing.

But what if there was? What if there was a place in her life for him, and he could be something to her? To someone else? He swallowed hard, barely letting himself think of the thing that could come next... Of kids.

It was a ridiculous thought. He had sent her the money, and he'd send her a way to find it. And then he would disappear.

Maybe he would check in on her now and then. But mostly... he'd just be gone.

That was his job, after all. Get in, get done, get gone.

Even when it hurt.

# EPILOGUE

Six months had passed since the cruise ship had finally docked, and Piper still felt a wash of apprehension whenever she walked into someplace even a little dark. It had taken her a month to walk down the street by herself. Marissa had stayed with her for weeks, helping her settle back into real life—and helping her find a therapist who could help her manage the stress of what had happened.

She'd had to edit a lot to talk about it without getting the police involved. Todd had left her alone, and Damian had promised her that would continue. The email that gave her instructions on how to access the account and the money he'd given her had also told her that there would be no way for him to contact her.

And her back ached, and her feet hurt, and she was absolutely exhausted all the time. She had never been so glad that her job involved mostly consulting from home, Skype calls, and webpage design. At least she could be exhausted and sore in her pajamas.

She didn't regret for a second the decision to have Damian's baby. Even if he would never know that it was happening. It felt like the right choice. That time on the cruise ship—it seemed like another lifetime. A movie that she remembered well. But there was more to it.

Just thinking of the way that he had tossed her around and made her soaking wet... She'd always heard that some women got higher libidos during pregnancy, but she'd never expected it to be like this. She'd burned out two vibrators thinking about the way he'd treated her. The sharp slaps on her ass, the vicious fucks, and the way he'd taken such sweet care of her afterward...

Marissa had finally dragged her out of the house for lunch, and as Piper walked back into her apartment, she felt that same rush of apprehension. She kept meaning to get someone to switch her apartment over to smart lighting so that she could turn the lights on before walking in, but she hadn't gotten to it yet.

She pushed the door open, flipped the switch next to the door, and then closed it behind her. There was a different feel to the apartment, and her heart started to race.

"Hello?" she called out, expecting the echoing silence that usually greeted her.

Instead, she heard light footsteps. A light flicked on in the living room. She drew in a breath to start screaming even as her throat tightened, and then she saw who was standing just ten feet from her.

"Damian?"

He was just as tall, rugged and handsome as he had been six months ago, but he'd grown out a light beard, and his hair was a little longer. He still radiated that same intensity, and she had a powerful memory, all through her body, of what it had felt like to feel him slam into her like it was where he'd always been destined to be.

"Hi, Piper," he said. His voice was light, soft, and she knew somehow that he was keeping it that way on purpose.

"What are you—Why are you—?" She was stuttering like a fool, and she hated it.

She took a deep breath, but the question wouldn't come to her lips. She wanted to run to him, kiss him, wrap him around her like the protector she knew he was—but she also knew that her pregnant belly was obvious now. And she couldn't take another step towards him until she knew what he was going to say about that.

"What am I doing here?"

She nodded. At least he was able to speak.

"I've... I don't want this to sound creepy, okay? Or at least, I'm hoping you can overlook the creepy factor." He took a deep breath and took one step closer to her.

She tried not to match it, either with a step forward or a step back. Impartial, that was her.

*Don't lie to yourself, Piper.*

She gave her inner monologue the finger and waited for him to continue.

"You were clear that you didn't want anything more to do with me, after—what happened. So I wanted to give you space. But despite what was said, I didn't truly believe that the Santiagos wouldn't use you to get to me. So I—I kept an eye on you. Not constantly—I wasn't watching you sleep or anything—but I watched out for you. I kept tabs, I guess."

"And?"

He was right, it did sound creepy, but she forced herself to breathe through the ick factor and focus on the caring that was hidden in those words. For a man like this to make sure she was safe showed something about how he felt for her. As far as he had ever told her, the only ever person he watched out for was his sister.

"Wait, I made it clear that I didn't want anything to do with you?"

His face twisted for a moment before he smoothed it back into its typical, calm expression. "That last night that we were together. I quite literally made you sick."

Piper was not a contract killer; she didn't know how to hide all of her emotions behind a wall and pretend they didn't exist. Her confusion showed, whether she wanted it to or not.

"What are you talking about?" And then it hit her. "You're talking about when I started vomiting."

He blinked hard, and she was sure that she'd startled him somehow.

"Yes?"

The uptick that made it into a question surprised her as well. She laughed; she didn't mean to, but the sound bubbled out of her before she could control it.

"I was—Morning sickness doesn't happen just in the morning, and you laid your arm over my stomach, and it just happened."

He went quiet, his eyes finally gliding down to focus on the roundness under her breasts. "It's... mine?"

"Yes," she said. It took a major effort of will not to add "you dolt," but she pulled it off.

"I... assumed it happened after you got back." He was perfectly still for a long moment, and she wasn't sure what to do or say. "Why didn't you say something?"

That was a very good question, and truthfully, one she had been dreading.

"I wasn't sure until—until we were at a spot where things were happening fast, and it was messy. I didn't think you should be distracted when you—" She realized that he'd been so careful with his language, and that was smart. The odds of someone surveilling her apartment were vanishingly small, but still. "You were busy."

"And that night?"

Now, she felt anger running through her. "When was I supposed to say something, between retches? And you were gone before I had even caught my breath."

He still hadn't moved. "And you decided to keep it, even though it was mine."

It was her turn to blink too fast. "Yes."

"Why?" There was something in that sound, a pain that had been buried for a very long time.

There was only one answer. She hadn't realized it until he left, and then she had no way to tell him.

"Because it's yours." She took a long, deep breath, then said the rest. "And because I love you."

He rocked back on his heels like she had slapped him. Her heart sank. It was too much to hope that he felt the same way, but all the times she'd allowed herself to think of this moment—which had been far more often than she'd thought was healthy or sane—he'd walked to her and pulled her into his arms.

Sometimes he had kissed her; sometimes he'd laid his hand over the swell of her belly with a quiet kind of possession that made her heart sing. Intellectually, she'd always known that his complete indifference, or even total disdain, had been possible. She just wished it wasn't like that.

"It's okay," Piper said as quickly as she could get the words out past the lump in her throat. With all the mental preparation that she had done for how this could go, she'd never imagined being so sad. "It's okay if you don't feel the same way. I just... You asked, so I needed to tell you."

"No, it's not… That's not it." He looked like he was wrestling with something deep inside of him, and she didn't know what it was.

She tried to watch and let it be, but the words wouldn't stay in her head.

"Why did you come here tonight?"

Why had he come into her darkened apartment when she clearly hadn't been home? Why had he waited for her? What had he thought would happen when he did this?

He took a long breath that sounded tight and maybe even a little bit afraid. "I had to see. I was sure it—that it wasn't mine. But I thought, what if it is?"

She let the hope surge through her. It might be dashed in a moment, but she had to let it be there. She didn't have a choice; it was that strong. "And now that you know?"

And then there was the moment she had let herself dream of, when she'd allowed herself to dream.

"I wanted it," he said, his voice barely a whisper. "I've always wanted it. From the moment I saw."

And then he stepped fast across the floor—she couldn't call it a run, she didn't dare—and he pulled her into his arms, pulling her face up to his for a vicious kiss that was full of want and a need for something so much more than just her mouth and her body.

She responded in kind, meeting every single motion of his lips and tongue. His hand stroked the curve of her belly, then slipped up to cup her heavy, swollen breasts, then swung down again to stroke what was now his. As soon as he had touched her, he'd claimed her. She knew it, inside and out. She would go anywhere and do anything he wanted.

"Mine." He snarled into her mouth and pushed her backward; it took her only a moment to realize that he was leading her towards the bedroom. "You're mine."

"I'm yours," she responded through the kisses.

"Forever. I'm keeping you forever."

"Yes," Piper said, with no hesitation. "Forever sounds perfect to me."

~

*Thanks for reading <u>ANDREI</u>! I hope you loved this bad boy mafia romance. If you are in the mood for some more deliciously dark romantic suspense, check out* The Dirty Dons Club: A Dark Mafia Romance Box Set!

*FIVE deliciously dark romantic suspense novels.*

*FIVE hair-raising, heart-clenching, screen-melting stories of love and hate, light and darkness, danger and passion.*

*FIVE dons with twisted imaginations and a never-ending appetite for MORE.*

Get ready to meet:

**SERGEI**

*A devil like me belongs nowhere near an angel like her.* Naomi was an innocent club girl. Hardly worth my time. But I needed a release, and so I claimed her the only way I know how: utterly and completely. And then I forgot about her. But she's back now—back in my underworld, back in my enemy's sights...and back with my accidental baby.

**LUCA**

*She didn't have my money. So I took her instead.* One way another, this debt is getting settled. Even if I have to claim her precious little body to make that happen. But when taking Anna causes more problems than it solves, I'm forced to answer one crucial question: How far will I go to protect my newest possession?

**VITO**

*She's drowning in the darkness. I'm here to pull her deeper.* My name is Vito Romano. I am everything they say I am: a killer, a criminal, a beast. Until I met her. I told myself I was rescuing Tammy. But we both know the truth: I took her to ruin her.

**NIKOLAI**

*I didn't plan to buy her. But once I had a taste, I couldn't let go.* Gabrielle is too pure to be up on that auction stage. But soon enough, I end up owning her. I'll show her that even though there is pain in the darkness... It's also full of pleasure. As long as she obeys me.

**ADRIK**

*I put my hands on her body. Nothing will ever be the same again.* Taylor saw me kill, and now I have no choice but to guarantee her silence. By any means necessary. From witness to fake wife in the blink of an eye. But when I begin to doubt she'll keep up her end of our dark bargain, I make my final move... And put a baby in her belly.

∽

**Get this bad boy bundle if you're ready for the midnight thrill of a lifetime!** Click here to start reading!

**Here's a sneak preview of Book 1, SERGEI:**

"Everything alright?" I ask. I'm in the VIP, so I have to lean in and ask loudly if I want the patrons to hear me. There are five people in the booth, four guys and one woman, the men dressed up in expensive-looking designer suits and the woman in—well, less than that.

"That'll be all," one of the men says to me. Forties, maybe, with really good hair and teeth, and the watch on his wrist looks ridiculously pricey. He hasn't given me his name but he's been flirting with me all night. He motions me over.

"I've never met you before. I come here a couple of times a month," he says over the thump of the music.

"We must have missed each other."

"Too bad. I would have loved to get to know you better. Here." He hands me a tip. I open my palm and it's a hundred-dollar bill. My eyes widen and I look back at him. "Hold on to that for me, 'til next time." He winks at me and I smile back.

Embers is a high-end night club in Midtown. Our clientele is mostly rich suits, their business partners, and the beautiful women they pay to keep around. I've been a bottle girl here for a few months and this nightlife gig isn't half bad. Better than I expected, at least. Especially when guys are forking over Benjamins because they think I'm cute.

The outfit does help, to be fair. Our uniform is tight, shimmery black dresses with plunging necklines and short hems. I think it's good with my hair, which I cut a while ago into a longish bob. The waves are natural but before work, I give them a little extra bounce with a curling iron.

One of my co-workers, Diana, is standing against the bar. I say hi and head around to the other side to restock my tray.

"Guess who just got a hundred-dollar tip," I tell her, with an excited little shimmy of my hips. Diana grins, leaning forward with her elbows on the bar.

"Very well done, Naomi," she says. It makes me laugh. She sounds like an elementary school teacher, which is the absolute opposite of her personality. "Was he hot?"

"Who?" I ask demurely, smiling but eyes down as I rinse a glass out.

"He *was*," she squeals, almost bouncing up and down.

I laugh. He probably was, depending on your definition of the term. Although, for Diana, a guy is only as hot as his net worth.

"Older. A suit. He's been flirting with me all night."

"Give him your number," she says.

"I have a fiancé, Di."

"He doesn't know that." She flips her long, blonde hair over her shoulder. "Besides, even if he did, he probably wouldn't care."

I nod, smiling because I don't like to judge. "*I* would."

She shrugs. "And that's why my boyfriend put down the money for a condo for me, myself, and I, and yours drives a 1993 Camry."

I raise my eyebrows. "Boyfriend?" I ask.

She shrugs. "He likes when I call him that. It's nicer than what he actually is."

"Which is what?"

Diana grins again, then looks down at her nails which are perfectly manicured. Her 'boyfriend' probably pays for that too. "A chump."

It's not hard to see why a man would spend his money on Diana. She is gorgeous, a busty blonde with a beguiling smile. 'Dating' men she meets here at the club when she is supposed to be working is her M.O. She is ruthless. None of them ever lasts longer than three or four months—plenty of time for her to rinse them for everything they are willing to hand over and move on to someone else. Funnily enough, they always chase after her even after she's run her game. The girl is intoxicating, I guess.

"Is he here tonight?" I ask.

"I told him to stop coming. I don't want him to distract me during work."

"Distract you from *what*? Pouring Jaeger bombs? Is that difficult?" I ask, giggling.

She scoffs. "Of course not. It's just hard to flirt with other guys when the one who thinks he's your boyfriend is watching."

I laugh and shake my head. She's a lot to handle, but I honestly learn so much from her about how to handle myself around here, even if what I learn isn't particularly good. It certainly isn't for the faint of heart. I wouldn't call myself a prude, but some of the stunts she pulls make my jaw drop.

I'm drying a few glasses off when I hear Diana say hi to someone. Angie, another bottle girl comes up to the bar, holding her empty tray to her chest.

"Hey, Ange," I say. Angie smiles at me across the bar. She's a tall brunette. Tonight, her hair is gathered away from her face in a high ponytail that makes her already-stunning bone structure even more arresting.

"Having a good night?" she asks.

"Angie, can you *please* tell Naomi to get the number of the hot businessman who has been flirting with her all night?" Diana interrupts.

"Angie, please tell Diana that serially dating guys from work is a bad idea."

Angie looks from Diana to me, then back to Diana. "She's right, Di. Where are your manners?"

"She's just jealous that my current man is a catch," Diana teases smugly. "Well, catch-and-release, I guess."

"*Current* man? Do these guys know how fast you cycle through them?"

"They're aware of the risks. I make 'em all sign a waiver before they get on the ride. Besides, who was the last guy *you* dated, Miss Love Doctor?"

"No, no, no. That's different."

"How?"

"They mean more to me than money and a couple of months of fun," she says.

"If you're looking for love, honey, you're looking in the wrong place. This is Embers, in case you're lost."

Angie shakes her head. "You don't know that. You never know where love can find you."

"If love is here, then it's *definitely* lost," Diana snorts.

"With that stank attitude, you're probably right." Di pretends to be offended as Angie looks at me. "Still, stank or not, Diana might be right. You should get his number. What could it hurt? Nothing wrong with a new friend, right?"

I balk. "What? No. C'mon, Ange, don't team up on me."

"You'll hate yourself for not doing it. You don't know. He might be the one."

"He's not the one, because I already found the one. I'm engaged, remember?" I protest. I would hold my hand up to flash the ring but I don't wear it while I'm working—availability, or at least the illusion of it, gets the tips. My fiancé, Jeremy, laughed at me the first time I went to him after work and told him that I was sorry for being friendly with customers because it felt like cheating. He likes that they can all look but they can't touch and I get paid for it.

"You don't need to do anything with him. Just make him *think* you will and he'll hook it up for you," Diana quips.

"Oh please. How long would that last?"

Diana shrugs. "A little side dick is good for the soul," she says. All three of us laugh, although I know she isn't really kidding.

They don't like Jeremy. My first night here, he picked me up after my shift and met both of the girls. Angie was polite to his face but told me later that she thought he wasn't in my league. Diana straight-up told him he was lucky I had such simple tastes.

I don't feel like I have to defend what I have with Jeremy. It works for us and that is all that matters. I will *not* be seeking out any 'side dick,' no matter how good it may or may not be for the soul.

Regardless, duty calls, so I load my tray and we disperse. I walk back over to the booth and start refreshing glasses and clearing away empty bottles as I ask around whether everyone is okay and if they need anything.

The guy who's been putting the moves on me all night motions me over again.

"Anything I can do for you?" I ask. I have to lean down to talk to him and, as I do, I see his eyes settle on my cleavage.

"Here," he says, holding out another tip. I take it and feel something strange. Wrapped in the bills is a card. His business card. "I want to see you again."

I smile at him. "That's flattering, thank you. If I see you again, can my fiancé come too?"

He looks mildly surprised at that, but not mad. He looks down and shakes his head. "If I say yes, will I see you again?"

I give him a tight smile and hold the card out to him. He takes it back.

"I had to give it a shot," he says. "Congratulations. He's a lucky guy."

I smile at him, grateful that he is taking the rejection so graciously. Many men don't know how to take no for an answer. They think the bottle girls are part of the merchandise, and well... actually, some of the girls kind of are.

But not me.

Click here to keep reading!

# MAILING LIST

Join the Naomi West Mailing List to receive new release alerts, free giveaways, and more!

Click the link below and you'll get sent a free motorcycle club romance as a welcome present.

JOIN NOW! http://bit.ly/NaomiWestNewsletter

# BOOKS BY NAOMI WEST

**Dark Mafia Kingpins**

Andrei

Leon

**Dirty Dons Club**

*Read in any order!*

Sergei

Luca

Vito

Nikolai

Adrik

**Bad Boy Biker's Club**

*Read in any order!*

Dakota

Stryker

Kaeden

Ranger

Blade

Colt

Tank

**Outlaw Biker Brotherhood**

*Read in any order!*

Devil's Revenge

Devil's Ink

Devil's Heart

Devil's Vow

Devil's Sins

Devil's Scar

**Box Sets**

Devil's Outlaws: An MC Romance Box Set

Bad Boy Bikers Club: An MC Romance Box Set

The Dirty Dons Club: A Dark Mafia Romance Box Set

**Other MC Standalones**

*\*Read in any order!*

Maddox

Stripped

Jace

Grinder

Printed in Great Britain
by Amazon